THE CURSE ON
SPECTACLE
KEY

THE CURSE ON SPECTACLE KEY

Chantel Acevedo

An Imprint of HarperCollinsPublishers

Balzer + Bray is an imprint of HarperCollins Publishers.

The Curse on Spectacle Key
 For information address HarperCollins Children's Books, a division of HarperCollins Publishers, 195 Broadway, New York, NY 10007.
www.harpercollinschildrens.com

Library of Congress Cataloging-in-Publication Data

Names: Acevedo, Chantel, author.
Title: The curse on Spectacle Key / Chantel Acevedo.
Description: First edition. | New York : Balzer + Bray, [2022] | Audience: Ages 8-12. | Audience: Grades 4-6. | Audience: Eleven-year-old Frank Fernández and his family move to Spectacle Key, Florida, where he befriends a ghost who needs Frank's help breaking the curse plaguing the island.
Identifiers: LCCN 2022000113 | ISBN 9780063134812 (hardcover)
Subjects: CYAC: Missing children--Fiction. | Memory--Fiction. | Lighthouses--Fiction. | Families--Fiction. | Cuban Americans--Fiction. | Mystery and detective stories. | Florida Keys (Fla.)--Fiction. | LCGFT: Novels. | Detective and mystery fiction.
Classification: LCC PZ7.A1733 Cu 2022 | DDC [Fic]--dc23
LC record available at https://lccn.loc.gov/2022000113

Typography by Joel Tippie
22 23 24 25 26 PC/LSCH 10 9 8 7 6 5 4 3 2 1
❖
First Edition

For Orlando, my beloved mad scientist

Chapter 1

READING BETWEEN THE LINES

The clock above the chalkboard ticked away the final few seconds of fifth grade. Around me, kids cleared out their desks, shoving books, old handouts, pencils, and notebooks into their backpacks until they were puffed up like pillows. All the while, my teacher, Ms. McCartney, shouted, "I want those desks CLEANED OUT, children!"

The room buzzed with excitement. We'd had a pizza party earlier, and Principal Hawkins even arranged for an ice-cream truck to give away Popsicles! At PE, Coach Rhodes set up a race where we put water balloons on our heads and tried to keep them from falling. The librarian, Ms. Parsons, handed out bookmarks, while Ms. Valdez, the art teacher, set up a splatter paint station in her classroom. Green paint had settled under my fingernails, and my hands looked like they belonged to a swamp monster.

Why didn't anybody tell me that the last day of school was the best day of the year?

I'd always missed it before because I'd be busy packing up my bedroom, getting ready to move to a new city or town thanks to my parents' work. But not this time. Mom and Papi had said we would stay in Auburn, Alabama, for another year, at least! I'd never been in one school for this long. It seemed that whenever I'd start making friends, we'd have to move again. Friendless Frank, that was me.

Around me, kids were discussing their summer plans. I overheard Lane talking about how his parents got him passes to the aquatic center in town. And Audrey was going on about her upcoming trip to Tennessee to visit her aunt. As for me, I had zero summer plans. Not that I minded. The fact that I didn't have anything to do was . . . amazing, actually.

No loading moving boxes into a truck in the summer heat. No unloading boxes either.

I leaned back in my desk chair and sighed happily.

Lane tapped my shoulder. "Hey, you, me, and the lazy river this summer, yeah?"

"Awesome!" I said. "Count me in!"

"All right, bro. See you later," he said with a laugh.

For most of the year, I'd kept to myself, expecting my parents to change their minds about staying in Auburn at any moment. But then one day Lane and I got grouped together for a science lab, and I noticed he had a comic book I'd read the year before at his desk, *The Legend of the Vampire Uncle.*

"That's a good one!" I'd told him. Lane went on about his collection of horror comics, while I told him about all the scary novels I had at home. On top of that, we aced the science lab. We both loved books, especially the ones that made you afraid to sleep alone at night, and we both thought science was the greatest subject in school.

If Dr. Frankenstein himself had built a perfect friend for me, based on the things I liked, then Lane would have been it. But I didn't let myself get too hopeful. My parents said we weren't moving *this* year. So I knew that living in Auburn wouldn't be a forever thing and at some point, I'd have to say goodbye again. Still, I was determined to enjoy my stay-at-home summer, and I was especially looking forward to not being the new kid in the fall for once.

The bell rang at last, and cheers filled the classroom. One by one, I watched as everyone pushed out of the room until it was just me and Ms. McCartney.

When I looked up, she was waving an envelope at me. I rushed to the front of the room to get it. It had my name on it, written in cursive.

"I think we both know what this is," Ms. McCartney said, giving me a wink.

My knees felt a little wobbly. Could it be?

I tore open the envelope and pulled out the letter. It read:

Dear Frank Fernandez,
It is with great pleasure that the Auburn

City Library admits you to its Junior Librarian Program! You'll get a chance to help organize our Summer Reading Bash, serve as a Reading Pal to a younger child, and meet visiting authors. At the end of the summer, you will get to choose three books of your own to keep!

Please sign and return the attached form to accept your spot in the program. Congratulations!

Keep reading,
Tonia Harrison
Librarian

"I can't believe it!" I shouted. I'd applied to the Junior Librarian Program back in the spring, reminding myself not to get my hopes up. I'd never applied to anything before, so in the "Experience" box of the application I'd had to write "None." As for the list of "Previous Schools Attended," I'd had to attach a separate sheet because there wasn't enough room on the form. But I thought my essay on my love of scary books was pretty good, and Ms. McCartney only had to correct about ten grammar errors.

Ms. McCartney gave me a fist bump. "Well done, Frank!"

"Thanks, Ms. M," I said, still grinning.

"I have something for you, by the way," she said, and started rummaging through the giant plaid bag she brought to class with her every day. I didn't know what to expect. One time, she pulled a basketball out of that bag when the one on the playground court deflated. She always had the perfect size Band-Aid in its depths, plus chargers for various devices. I'd seen a power drill, an inflatable Santa Claus, and even a stray calico kitten come out of there. Someone would always whisper "Mary Poppins" whenever she started digging into it. With Ms. McCartney, anything was possible.

"Aha!" she said at last, and handed me a heavy brass magnifying glass. The glass had a sculpted wooden handle, and engraved in the brass it read: *For reading between the lines.*

"Between the lines?" I asked, turning the object in my hand.

Ms. McCartney nodded. "When you read between the lines, you understand more than just what the words mean. You understand what the author was trying to *really* say. How they were hoping to tap into your brain and your heart. When you read between the lines, you notice patterns, and where there is a pattern, there is meaning. Read between the lines, Frank, and you won't go wrong."

I didn't entirely understand what Ms. M was trying to tell me, but I loved her gift anyway. An antique-looking magnifying glass seemed like just the kind of thing a real librarian would have in their desk!

"Thanks, Ms. M. I love the magnifying glass. See you in the library this summer?"

Ms. McCartney smiled. "You bet. You'll find me in the

horror section, between the ghosts and the werewolves. Deal?"

"You got it!" I said. Just like Lane, Ms. M and I had the same taste in books. When I left the classroom, my cheeks were aching from smiling so much.

For the first time ever, my summer would consist of fun things, not boxes and moving trucks. Not only was I going to go to the pool with Lane a bunch of times, but I'd get to volunteer at the library, which was my favorite place in the world. There would be tons of books to read, maybe even new friends to make.

I would be Friendless Frank no more!

I had never, *ever* been happier.

Chapter 2

GOODBYE, TRAIN STATION

My family lived in a converted train station right in the middle of town. It had high ceilings and the brass ticket booth still standing in one corner where I'd pretend to buy train tickets to anywhere and everywhere. Papi had found the station so he and Mom could renovate it and turn it into a home. Before my parents came along, the ceiling was caved in, and college kids used to sneak in at night to throw parties. But Mom and Papi had turned it into a beautiful house, the kind people put in magazines and, more importantly, buy from my parents. Their business, Fernández Home Conversions, was dedicated to taking unusual structures and turning them into great homes for families to buy.

The renovation wasn't done yet, which was why we were sticking around in Auburn for another year. The front door still stuck, for example, so I had to kick the door while wiggling the key at the exact same time for it to open. It wasn't an easy thing to do with a backpack full of books, paper, old projects, and school supplies. I couldn't wait to tell Mom and Papi about Lane's passes to the aquatic center and the Junior Librarian Program!

As soon as I walked inside, I heard my mom call, "Mister, we need to talk." At first, I wondered if I'd left my stinky PE shoes in the middle of the hall again. Papi tripped on them last week and I'd gotten a huge lecture on putting my things away.

"Hijo, come here," Papi said softly, and my stomach dropped. Oh no. This wasn't about the shoes. I knew what was coming, and it never got easier.

"When?" I demanded, flinging my loaded backpack onto the kitchen table. Papi had made the table out of railway ties, with strong iron clasps holding it together. A team of people could barely lift it.

"Oh, mister," Mom said sadly.

Papi wandered into the kitchen, blueprints rolled up under his arm. "Wait till you see our next project, Junior. You're going to love it."

"I doubt it. I love *this* place," I said, sitting at the table and hiding my face in my hands. I mumbled through my fingers. "I like living in Alabama. And I was going to hang out with Lane this summer! We made plans and everything. Besides," I added, "you said this renovation would take longer than the others. You said I'd get to have two years in one school! You said so!" I stopped talking when my voice started to quiver. One of the bathrooms was still incomplete, and the backyard was torn up. Why were we leaving this place already?

Mom and Papi pulled chairs up to the table, their legs screeching against the concrete floor. "I know, hijito," Papi was saying. "We have a buyer eager to move in and finish the renovation on his own. Plus, an opportunity came up that we can't pass on. You know the deal. This is how we make a living."

I slid the Junior Library Program letter across the table, keeping my eyes closed as my parents read it silently.

"Ay, Junior," Papi said with a sigh. "I'm sorry."

"Unless the next home conversion is in a library full of books, I don't want to hear it," I complained. I loved books the way my parents loved renovating places to live. They'd transformed an old schoolhouse in Pittsburgh, a church in upstate New York, a water tower in Atlanta, even a car repair shop in New Haven all into amazing houses. We'd lived in each of the places my parents renovated, so my whole life had been one big construction site. I was used to dusty rooms, stepping on nails (I always wore shoes indoors), Porta-Potties for when the bathrooms didn't work—and living in the coolest house in town.

I still thought about Mikey in Pittsburgh, Valentina in New York, and Jerome in Atlanta. They'd all promised to keep in touch, but none of us had cell phones yet, and, well, moving day was the last I'd seen of them. So when I got to New Haven, and later Dallas, Mission Viejo, and Saint Paul, I'd made up my mind not to make any new friends.

And now I'd let my guard down and gotten my hopes up. I'd made a friend, and even worse, made *plans* with that friend. Plus, I'd applied to a summer program and gotten in. Shouldn't have done that either. Then there was Ms. McCartney, the best teacher I'd ever had. If I hadn't become Lane's friend, or applied to the Junior Librarian Program, or gotten to know Mrs. M so well, I wouldn't be feeling so awful about moving. Auburn would be just another pushpin in the map of places we'd left behind.

Why had I believed my parents when they'd told me we'd be sticking around this time?

I felt Mom's hand on the top of my head. "But we've got good news," she said.

"Actually," Papi put in, "there are three pieces of good news."

"You're right," Mom said. "Which do you want first, mister? The good news, the good news, or the good news?"

I pretended to think for a minute. "Um, I'll take the good news, I guess."

"¡Perfecto!" Papi announced. He rolled out the blueprints in front of me. What I saw made my jaw drop.

"A lighthouse? You're renovating a lighthouse?" The line drawings showed a tall structure with a spiraling staircase inside. Each floor had its own room, with the kitchen and living room downstairs on the ground level. I hated to admit it, but it looked awesome.

"¡Sí, señor!" Papi said.

Mom's eyes were shiny and her cheeks were glowing. I'd never seen her look so happy about a new place. "I took one look at the advertisement and I just *knew* we had to renovate the place. It was like I felt it in my bones," Mom said. "There was a competing offer, but we won the bid."

"Meant to be!" Papi added.

"And it's our last move. I promise. From now on, the lighthouse on Spectacle Key will be our base of operations."

I shrugged. I'd been so excited when they'd promised we would get to stay in Alabama for a little longer. I wanted to believe them, but could I? "Yeah, right. You said we would stay in Auburn for two years."

Mom and Papi looked at each other. Sometimes I thought they were communicating telepathically.

"This time it's different," Mom said.

"We promise," Papi added.

No more moving? I thought, hardly believing it. I rolled my eyes, which would normally get me in trouble, but Mom and Papi let it slide.

"And do you know why it's different this time?" Mom asked.

I shook my head.

"Well, can you guess where Spectacle Key is?" Mom went on.

I wondered for a moment. It had to be near the ocean, of course. East Coast or West Coast, though? I took a stab at it. "North Carolina," I guessed.

"Close," Papi said. "Head south."

"Florida!" I exclaimed. My heart started pounding. If we were moving to Florida, that meant we were going to be closer to my pop-pop, who lived in Miami.

Mom clapped. "The Florida Keys, to be specific. You got it in two!" she said.

Suddenly, I felt as if I could float. Pop-Pop! He was the greatest pal in the world. There was nobody like my grandfather. Plus, if we were staying in one place, for real this time, then maybe I'd get to make new friends my own age. Maybe I'd make a *best* friend, somebody I would know for years and years.

"We're going home, Frank. *Home*," Mom said, her eyes shining.

My mom grew up in the Keys. Technically, she's from Key Largo. We didn't visit that often, though. Nobody in the family lived there anymore. My cousins were scattered all over the country, having gotten away from the heat and the hurricanes as soon as they could.

"And I'll be closer to mi país, too," Papi added.

My dad was from Cuba, and the Keys were only ninety miles away from the island he had left when he was a kid.

"Home," I repeated.

"Home," my parents said at the same time. Suddenly, the

Junior Library Program seemed a little less important. My heart still clenched when I thought of Lane, though. He was the coolest kid I'd ever met. It stung to think about missing out on the Auburn summer I'd planned, but . . . I'd never have to move again. That was the best news I'd had all day. It was the best news *ever,* in fact.

Mom looked up Spectacle Key on her phone and showed me the website she found. "Spectacle Key is one of many small islands that make up the Florida Keys all the way at the end of the state. *Key* is just another word for island. The key we'll be living on is called Spectacle Key because it's in the shape of a pair of glasses. The lighthouse sits on one of the 'lenses,'" she read out loud.

"What's on the other lens?" I asked. A picture of Spectacle Key had already started forming in my brain. Water all around, palm trees, warm weather, Pop-Pop nearby. It sounded like a dream.

"An abandoned, run-down building," Papi said. "It came with the lighthouse. Maybe we'll convert that one, too."

"Don't get too excited," Mom warned him. "The keys are all connected by one street and a series of bridges. One road in, one road out," she added. "And Pop-Pop will be just two hours away by car. He's getting older, and it's time we moved closer to him."

Pop-Pop lived in Miami, where he had been a professor of chemistry at the university. When he gets going on his theories about nanotechnology or molecular structures, he sounds like a cross between a mad scientist and a wizard. I missed him like crazy.

"Good news numero tres is . . ." Papi drummed on the table while Mom jumped up and ran to the laundry room, putting her hand on the door handle.

"You always say it's hard to make friends," she said, her voice cracking a bit like she was getting weepy. I looked down at my hands. It didn't feel so great to be reminded of how lonely I was at times. "And your papi and I know how difficult all this moving has been for you. So to make it up to you, and to make sure you always have a friend nearby, we got you this." Mom slowly opened the door to the laundry room and beckoned me over with her finger.

I got up quietly and joined her. On the floor, sleeping on a cushion and curled up like a snail, was the biggest puppy I had ever seen. Its paws were already the size of my hand, which meant this wouldn't just be a big dog. This would grow up to be a *huge* dog!

"For me?" I asked, and now it was my turn to have a cracking voice.

Mom and Papi nodded. "She's all yours. And she's a Great Dane, which means she'll have the run of Spectacle Key in no time," Mom added.

The puppy was gray with black spots and long lashes. When she opened her eyes, she looked at me sleepily, then, realizing that there was someone new to play with, she bounded up and jumped on me. Her front paws reached my shoulders.

I was 100 percent in love with her already.

"We are going to be the bestest friends," I whispered, and gave her a hug. The dog licked me all over, covering me in stinky puppy breath. We'd . . . have to work on that.

"What are you going to name her?" Mom asked.

I had the answer immediately.

"Mary Shelley."

"The author of *Frankenstein*? Por supuesto," Dad said with a sigh.

Frankenstein is my favorite story, not because my name is Frank (and yes, I've heard *that* joke about a million times), but because of the monster that Dr. Frankenstein created. He was huge, green, and made up of different human parts, plus he didn't have any friends.

If that last part sounds familiar, it's because it was.

It was Pop-Pop who gave me my first copy of *Frankenstein* for my tenth birthday. On the cover of the book was a picture of a man holding a lantern over his head. Behind him, books and lab equipment littered a dungeon-like room. Before him, a body was laid out on a wooden table, with only the giant, veiny feet visible. It was horrifying.

And I was obsessed with it.

The novel is abridged, which means it's shorter than the original story, and easier to read. I've read it more times than I can count, and told everyone I knew how cool it was, so now, when I have a birthday, or Christmas rolls around, I get *Frankenstein* stuff. My collection is pretty cool. I have a couple of Frankenstein comic books, a bunch of action figures, as well as two posters—one of the 1931 movie, and one of *The Bride of Frankenstein*.

Pop-Pop thought I would enjoy the story because it was spooky, but also because of the science bits, which would remind me of him. He was right, of course. He usually is.

Mary Shelley bounded out of the laundry room and chased me all over the train station. I put her leash on and we played outside. Every once in a while, college kids would stop and coo at her. When they'd ask me her name and I told them, they'd give me a weird look.

It was okay. I wouldn't be living in a college town in Alabama for much longer.

Me and Mary Shelley were moving to a lighthouse with my folks, and it was going to be amazing.

Chapter 3

WELCOME TO SPECTACLE KEY

We took a week to pack up the train station and say goodbye to Auburn, which wasn't easy. Goodbyes never are. But I did get one epic day at the aquatic center with Lane, ate barbecue for lunch afterward, and then he came over to play with Mary Shelley for a while.

"Can I visit you in Florida?" Lane asked.

"Of course!" I told him. "It's going to be so awesome living in a lighthouse."

Lane's eyes grew wide. "Yeah. And probably really scary, too."

"Huh?" I asked.

Lane nodded wisely. "The scariest place to be on a dark and stormy night is not a castle or a cabin in the woods. It's a *lighthouse*. They get struck by lightning all the time.

Sometimes lighthouses wash away, and the people inside are lost forever. And lighthouses are usually haunted. That's a fact."

"You're making stuff up," I said.

Lane crossed his boots at the ankles. "Nope. I know things, man." Then he busted out laughing. "Just kidding. You're gonna have such a great life!"

I got a little choked up having to say goodbye, so I gave Lane my whole collection of *Vampire Uncle* comics instead of getting sappy or weird. Lane must have felt the same way, because we just fist-bumped silently and then he went home without actually saying anything.

Like I said, goodbyes are hard, and sometimes, they're really awkward.

Soon enough, the day came when we had to pile into my parents' van, loaded with our suitcases, and drive eleven hours to get to the very southernmost part of Florida. To reach Spectacle Key, we had to drive on US 1, the single road that leads in and out of the Florida Keys. In some places, the road gets very narrow, and the water on either side is so close you could jump out of the car window for a splash. In others, US 1 widens to a few lanes, but still never gets too large. We passed key after key, each with lots of little hotels inviting guests in with their colorful, blinking signs, and plenty of touristy shops selling seashells and airbrushed T-shirts. My favorite was hand-painted and read:

The sign was in the form of an eyeball with lashes jutting out like hairy spider legs. I couldn't believe anybody actually went to see a psychic. Pop-Pop always said that the best approach to a problem is a logical one. And there was nothing at all logical about somebody claiming to see into the future, speak to ghosts, or tell your fortune from a set of cards. Still, the part of me that loved scary books was intrigued by Mama Z's sign. Whoever she was, I bet she had spooky stories to tell. Several billboards with the same picture on them caught our attention, too, and Mom, Papi, and I counted out loud every time we saw one.

"Another one! That's five!" Mom shouted.

"Otro más," said Papi, halfway to Spectacle Key.

"There she is again!" I cheered, and Mary Shelley howled beside me. It was a billboard featuring a woman with very blond hair in a short bob. She had a big, cheesy smile, wore a superhero cape billowing behind her, and was holding a paintbrush. Beside her, as if she'd painted the sign herself, were the words:

EMILY SHIVERTON FOR THE FLIPPY AWARD!
THE FLORIDA KEYS' NUMBER ONE DEFENDER!

"What's a Flippy Award?" I wondered.

Papi laughed and shrugged. "No idea. I was warned that the Florida Keys are a little bit weird. I guess that's the kind of thing we should expect," he said.

"Not weird. Quirky!" Mom added. "The Flippies are a big deal around here! They honor people who make good contributions to life on the Keys. Maybe we'll win one someday."

We stopped for a bathroom break at a café selling fish tacos. Mom said they were the best she'd ever had, and Papi grumbled happily as he chewed. The café had a gift shop where my parents bought me a book called *Haunted Places in the Florida Keys*.

"Right up your alley, I think," Papi said, handing me the book at the register. I couldn't wait to read it! Mom and Papi got matching I ♥ Florida T-shirts, and I used my allowance to get a chew toy for Mary Shelley in the shape of a seashell.

"Next stop—home!" Mom announced, and we climbed back into the van for the last leg of the trip.

An hour later, we found the entrance to Spectacle Key and turned onto the island. It was raining, and Papi got the windshield wipers going. Mom grumbled about not having any umbrellas in the car, while Mary Shelley passed so much gas beside me that I had to open a window, which got me soaked.

"Talk about starting off on the wrong foot," Mom said. Papi drove along the gravel road that led to our new home.

The broken signs pointing the way were no help, but it was okay. You couldn't miss the lighthouse, which stood gray and stark in the distance. Finally, we arrived. The rain slowed to a trickle, and we all got out of the van.

Standing in front of the actual lighthouse made me realize there was a reason Mom and Papi got a good deal on the place.

A couple of reasons, in fact.

We gazed up at the lighthouse—Mom, Papi, Mary Shelley, and me—on what felt like the most humid day of the year. Mom's hair was puffed up like cotton candy. Papi jiggled the keys to the front door nervously in one hand.

"It looked like it was in better shape in the pictures," Mom said, pointing at cracks up and down the side.

"It's probably got a great interior," Papi said cheerfully.

"Hmm," Mom said. "Looks like a money pit."

Papi scowled at her. "What do we always do when life gives us lemons?"

"Complain about the lemons," Mom mumbled.

It took Papi several minutes to get the key to actually fit into the lock, and he grunted and cursed the whole time, sweating up a storm. Beside me, Mary Shelley, who seemed to grow several inches per day, panted and whined. At last the door creaked open, and we peered into the dark space within.

Mom walked in first, feeling the walls for the light switch. When she finally flipped it on, the overhead lights sputtered to life. A bulb exploded, popping like a balloon and showering us with the shards of glass. I jumped at the sound, and Mary Shelley tried to run back to the van in fear, yanking me three feet in that direction.

Mom shook her fist at the ceiling, as if the light bulb had personally attacked her. I held tight to Mary Shelley's collar so that she wouldn't get any slivers in her paws as Papi cleaned up the mess.

While everyone was busy, I took the time to drink in the rest of the lighthouse, scanning it all the way to the top. There wasn't a straight line in the place. The lighthouse was a giant cylinder, and it felt like being inside a humongous worm. The staircase went up and up like a spine, slicing through floor after floor until it reached the top, where the huge lantern sat like an eye blazing over the sea.

Papi caught me looking and his eyes twinkled. "It's time for some vertical explorations!" he said, charging up the stairs. I ran up after him. "This'll be your room, Junior," Papi announced, opening a door on the third floor. The walls were a weird brown color and the floors creaked, but the view of the ocean blew me away. In the distance, I could see the abandoned building my parents had mentioned, the one that sat on the other "lens" of Spectacle Key. The sun glinted off the roof, and it must have hit it in a certain way because my room suddenly filled with a burst of light that came and went quickly, and the four of us, including my dog, squeezed our eyes shut.

"What in the world was that?" Mom asked, rubbing her eyes.

"Must be something reflective on the roof of that ruin," Papi said, squinting into the distance.

"Speaking of lights," I said, and pointed up. We were in a lighthouse, after all! Which meant that at the very top of this thing was a lamp. It was a decommissioned lighthouse, so boaters no longer depended on it to navigate their way around the Keys—but that didn't mean we couldn't turn on the light.

"Let's go!" Papi said, laughing like a kid and running up to the top of the lighthouse. He froze on the last step. "Oh no," I heard him say as the ginormous lamp came into view.

I'd bought a book from one of the turnpike rest stops. It was all about lighthouses up and down Florida's coast. They didn't list the one on Spectacle Key, which was a bummer, but I did learn a lot about how they work. A lighthouse lamp, called a Fresnel lens, is made of glass that has been shaped with rings into its surface. It looks sort of like a huge crystal thumbprint. But the lamp at the top of our lighthouse was dingy, and a long crack was visible along the length of it.

Mom and Papi inspected the crack. "I think it can still work," Papi said at last. "The crack is very fine."

The rest of the equipment up there was rusty and full of sand, as if the wind had been blowing the beach up into the lighthouse for years. I guess it probably had. We were all a little defeated after the tour of our new home, so Mom and

Papi decided to focus on getting settled and worry about the renovations another day.

The truth was, there was plenty to worry about.

I went up to my bedroom to start unpacking. I started with the books, of course. There was a set of shelves built right into the wall. They were dusty and covered with lizard droppings, but a quick sweep meant they were ready to hold my favorite books. "No more dark moving boxes for you," I said to the copy of *Frankenstein* Pop-Pop gave me, and set it first on the shelf.

I tried hanging my clothes up in my closet, but there was green, bumpy mold in all the corners.

"Ew," I said out loud, and Mary Shelley sniffed and whined. A crab spider crawled into a corner of the closet, touched the mold with one leg, then curled up and fell, twitching, on the floor near my foot.

"That's probably not a good thing," I muttered to myself, picking up the dead crab spider and tossing it out the window. My clothes could wait. Mary Shelley was lying on her back now and waving her paws in the air just like the crab spider, except Mary Shelley was just being goofy and not poisoned by mold. That's when the electricity in my bedroom flickered, and suddenly my room looked like a scene in a horror movie just before the monster surprises their victim for the last, deadly time.

"This place is a disasterpiece," I said to Mary Shelley. A

mouse scurried out of the closet just then, and I leaped onto my bed and did a whole-body shiver. On its way out, the mouse gave me a look that said *I can't believe anybody moved in here* before running down the stairs.

Maybe the mouse knew something we didn't. Spooked now, Mary Shelley and I followed the mouse and left my creepier-by-the-minute bedroom.

I went to look for my parents to report on the mold, the spider, and the mouse.

"Hey, you won't believe what I just—" I started to say, but Mom interrupted me.

"It's rank," Mom said, turning up her nose. "We've fixed some whoppers, hun, but this one has them all beat."

Papi scowled. "This lighthouse is a palace! Back in Cuba, we were so broke that I lived in una ratonera!" he said as he loaded our stuff inside, comparing his old, cramped apartment in Havana to a rat's nest.

I decided not to tell them about the mouse in the closet.

Mom muttered, "We should've stayed in the train station a little longer."

"Where's your sense of adventure, Joyce?" Papi asked her, hammer in hand, as he drove loose nails back into the steps on the staircase.

"Must have left it back in Alabama," Mom answered. Mary Shelley started snapping at the air, as if some tiny, invisible thing was bugging her.

"Quit it, girl," I said.

Mom gave Mary Shelley a pat on the head. "You don't like this place either, do you?" she asked.

Papi whirled on us. "No more complaining. Fernándezes don't complain—we get to work. This is home, like we planned, Joyce. Home, para siempre. I'm tired of moving. We all are. I want to be taken out of this lighthouse in a pine box!"

Under her breath, Mom muttered, "Like I'd even pay for pine."

It was as if the lighthouse had cast a grumpy spell on my parents. They were *used* to fixing old dumps. They'd managed all kinds of disasters, always with a laugh and a hug for one another at the end of the day. Why was the lighthouse any different?

Maybe the problem was that we wouldn't be moving again. The lighthouse was it. Forever. Maybe the idea of that stressed them out. As for me, I was glad. So what if the lighthouse was broken, stinky, and uncomfortable? I never had to pack another box again. I was home. HOME. In my bedroom, I piled up more books on my nightstand, since the bookshelf was quickly filled. I arranged the books in A-B-C order, then tried doing it by color, and finally settled on organizing them by "fright factor." It was summer now, but come the fall, I'd be a sixth grader. After a year, I wouldn't be the new kid ever again. By then I'd make friends—friends who would probably think that living in a lighthouse was the coolest thing ever.

That night, Mom, Papi, and I ordered takeout from a

restaurant on the neighboring key. We had conch fritters and Key lime pie. "A real Keys dinner!" Mom had said, and told us about fishing for red snapper with Pop-Pop when she was a little girl, and how kids on the mainland teased her and called her "key rat" growing up, but how it didn't matter, because growing up on an island chain was the best kind of childhood there was.

That's when the ceiling fan in the living room decided to give up the ghost, crashing to the ground and splintering in a thousand pieces. Papi threw his hands in the air and shouted, "¡Ay!" which startled Mary Shelley and made her pee under the table. Thankfully, we were in the kitchen at the time, otherwise someone could have been seriously hurt.

"The lighthouse strikes again," Mom said once everyone's hearts stopped pounding.

"Accidents happen," Papi said, trying to be cheerful.

"They seem to happen here a lot," Mom muttered.

"Not this again—"

I excused myself from the table and went upstairs. It was dark outside, and the wind was squealing through the gaps in the window. I could feel the air snaking into my room. I curled up with Mary Shelley on my bed, settling down for the night. She took up more than half the space and snored like a fork stuck in a garbage disposal once she fell asleep.

Outside, the wind picked up, and a sweet smell filled the room. The moon was full and bright, and it cast a blue light over Spectacle Key. I scratched behind Mary Shelley's ears, and she nuzzled closer. Downstairs, my parents had gone quiet, too.

"Moving day is always rough," I whispered to myself, remembering all those other places I'd lived. Something always went wrong. "Tomorrow is going to be much better." Exhausted, I fell dead asleep.

Chapter 4

DING-DONG-DITCH

The next day, just before dinnertime, there was a knock on the door.

"Get that, will you, Frankie?" Mom called from deep inside the kitchen pantry, where she was stacking canned food. She kept talking about all the hurricanes she remembered on the Keys when she was growing up, so we were up to our eyeballs in cans of gross veggies, batteries, and bottled water.

I stomped down the staircase, hopping over the one step with the crack down the middle, and ran to the door. Mary Shelley crowded me on the stairs until I let her pass, then she flopped onto the last two steps and decided to take a nap. I jumped over her and opened the door—but no one was there. I scanned the walkway to the lighthouse for a moment, but the only things I saw were the palm trees that lined it, flapping wildly in the stiff ocean breeze.

I closed the door, took a few steps back into the lighthouse, then heard knocking again.

"Mary Shelley, here, girl," I said, nervous now. Not that she would ever hurt a person, but she was so huge she'd intimidate anyone. Except Mary Shelley only opened one eye when I called her name. She looked at me for a second before falling right back asleep.

Worst guard dog ever, I thought. Whoever it was knocked over and over again, in a heartbeat rhythm. My own heart thudded wildly. Knocking like that was a creepy thing to do for sure. I grabbed an umbrella from the stand beside the door, ready to swing it at someone if necessary. I took a deep breath and yanked open the door, hoping to be quick enough to catch whoever had decided to play "ding-dong-ditch" on me.

"Gotcha!" I shouted.

But again, nobody was there. I took a step outside and the air felt warm, and so humid it was thick enough to slice with a knife. Even so, the hairs on my arms stood on end, like they do when it's chilly. I waited there for a minute or two, listening to the palms knocking together and the waves crashing ashore in the distance. That's when I heard it.

A sigh.

"Who's there?" I whispered. A fruity scent filled the air. There were fruit trees all over the island—mango, papaya, guanabana, banana. Maybe that's where the smell was coming from?

Then I heard it again, another sigh, soft as a cat's purr, and with it that same sweet smell. Mom called my name, making me jump a foot in the air, then both the sound and aroma disappeared.

I stood there for a minute before shutting the door. In the books I read, this was usually the part when one of the minor characters decides to follow the sound or the smell, and always ends up possessed by ghosts, or taken by vampires, or on the menu at a swamp monster's deli. Not the main character, though—the main character always thinks things through a little more carefully.

I'm no side character, I decided.

"Frankie! Don't make me wear out your name, mister!"

"Yes, ma'am," I called, closing the door and joining Mom in the kitchen. There were boxes everywhere. Mom had pulled the ancient oven back from the wall to reveal a cemetery of dried-out lizards, bees, and roaches. She handed me a broom. "Be my knight in shining armor, will you, Frankie?"

"Ew," I muttered, and got to work, sweeping all the dead things out from behind the oven.

"Who was at the door?" Mom asked as she watched me work. She opened a can of orange soda and gulped it down. Sweat ran down her temples.

"Nobody," I answered, just as a real live lizard skittered over my feet and dashed for a new dark corner to inhabit.

Mom stopped mid-swallow and sputtered. "Nobody?"

"Nope," I said. "I think someone was playing ding-dong-ditch."

"Who would be on the key besides us?" Mom wondered. She grabbed a new orange soda from the fridge and handed it to me, then peered out the window as if she might catch whoever was playing a prank on us. "We might could've just moved to Miami Beach," she muttered to herself.

Whenever Mom said "might could've" instead of just plain "could have," I knew she was frustrated. I brushed the last of the dead things onto a dustpan.

"At least it wasn't one of those Historical Association of Unique National Treasures people," Mom said casually, as if she hadn't just rattled off the longest proper noun in the history of proper nouns.

"The Historical what now?" I asked. A dead lizard fell out of the dustpan and landed on the stove.

Mom took a deep breath. "They're called HAUNT for short. It's a group that's very interested in our moving here. They've got a bee in their bonnet about the lighthouse being 'a particularly important building of interest,' or some such thing. Guess who their president is?"

I shrugged.

"Ms. Emily Shiverton!"

"The Flippy lady?" I asked. I couldn't believe she was a real person!

"Well, I told Ms. Flippy herself that we were just going to

live in the lighthouse and get that lamp going again. She left in a huff. You missed her visit earlier this morning. Eight a.m. is not a decent hour to go knocking on somebody's door."

We heard a clatter coming from upstairs, and Papi started cursing.

"If it's not one thing, it's another. I'd better see what's going on up there," she said with a roll of her eyes. She wiped a dribble of orange soda off my cheek.

"C'mon, Mary Shelley," I said as I started to climb the stairs behind Mom. Mary Shelley stood, shook her huge gray head, and sent drool flying everywhere before following. The stairs curled up the side of the wall, past the second floor, where my parents' bedroom was, past the third, where my room sat, beyond the fourth, where they'd set up a TV room, and then to the top, where the lamp was.

"Me caso en la madre de—" Papi was saying when we got to the top. He stopped just short of cursing when he saw that we'd joined him.

"What happened now?" Mom asked.

"First of all, my favorite hammer has gone missing. Just up and disappeared. Yesterday it was a screwdriver, and this morning my *second*-favorite hammer went missing. And mira," Papi said, pointing to the crack in the lamp's glass, which seemed to have gotten even longer.

Mom whistled. "The hits just keep on coming." Papi shot her a look, but he bit his tongue.

"Can you fix it?" I asked.

Papi shook his head. "I don't know, Frank."

Mom walked around the lamp, her fingers touching the glass lightly. "Such a pretty girl. I wish we could make her shine again," she said with a sigh.

I jumped as Papi slammed his toolbox shut.

"I'm trying, okay," he said.

"I didn't mean to suggest—" Mom started to explain. But Papi brushed past us both, his toolbox banging against the stair's handrails as he went.

Mom and I stood there beside the dead lamp. Outside, the sea churned angrily, and dark clouds gathered, as if the whole world felt the way we did—frustrated and sad.

"I should start dinner," Mom said. "Go take a break upstairs, mister. If you read, turn your light on. I'll make meat loaf for dinner, okay?"

"Okay," I said.

My bedroom window was open, and I could smell the sea, salty and thick. It had started to rain. It seemed to rain on the island all the time, but when I'd look at the weather app on my mom's phone, the other keys were bone dry. Just our luck, we moved to the rainiest island in the Keys. There was a new stack of scary novels on my nightstand, courtesy of Pop-Pop, who knew what I liked. I propped one open—*The Bloody Plumber*—and tried to read. But I couldn't concentrate. Mom and Papi were arguing about the cost of a new air conditioner downstairs, and I could hear them clearly. Plus, there was a scratching sound right behind me. Papi was sure we had a colony of bats making their home in the lighthouse walls. I closed the book and looked out to where the lonely, abandoned building sat. A light flashed in one of the windows. There and gone so fast I thought that I had imagined it.

I remembered the ding-dong-ditcher and Papi's missing tools, and a thought settled over me, cold as an ice cube shoved down the back of my shirt.

What if that run-down place isn't *empty?*

I shuddered and slammed my window shut, just in case.

Chapter 5

A NAME IN THE SAND

In the morning, I took Mary Shelley out on a long walk, keeping close to the lighthouse. I didn't use a leash, because Mary Shelley was a good dog and because there wasn't ever anybody but us around. She usually stayed by me, nosing me in the ribs if she thought I was walking too slowly.

My left pocket was stuffed with old plastic grocery bags tied into knots to pick up her giant poops. Cleaning up after a Great Dane is no joke. If a genie ever showed up during our walks, I'd probably waste one of my three wishes turning Mary Shelley into a Chihuahua.

Less food in, less you-know-what out.

In my right pocket, I carried a fistful of candy. Mom always said I had a "tooth so sweet it gives cavities to people *near* you, mister." Cavities shmavities. Who could resist a deliciously chewy caramel? Or a glossy, perfect gummy bear?

Mary Shelley took her time, sticking her wet nose in the tall grass and ducking under the sea grape bushes to spook the raccoons that made their nests down there. She sniffed around the base of the lighthouse, as if some other dog, long ago, had left a mark. Mainly, she lumbered this way and that, barked at nothing, and didn't stray too far.

But then, out of the blue, Mary Shelley stuck her nose up in the air and *bolted*.

"Mary Shelley! Come on, girl!" I cried, chasing her. My feet pounded the sand and I got tangled up in dry weeds. My arm caught on a beautyberry vine, and when I shook it loose, a hundred tiny purple berries showered the ground. I jumped over a low gumbo-limbo branch, then had to duck under the next one. The whole time, Mary Shelley was getting farther away. The only thing I could see was her tail, whipping the grasses.

When I finally stopped, I had to bend over, resting my hands on my knees. Looking up, I saw that Mary Shelley had stopped, too. Before us was the abandoned ruin. It was a large stone building, two stories tall. Except half of the top story was open, as if a giant had come and taken a huge bite out of the top of the house. The bottom half rested on four arched doorways, so the place seemed to be standing on many clawed feet.

If this were a nightmare, that building would have totally come alive to devour me and Mary Shelley.

"Come on, let's go home," I whispered, not wanting to be near the creepy ruin any longer. But when I pulled on Mary Shelley's collar, she wouldn't budge. She looked up at me with her big, wet, brown eyes, blinked twice, and whined.

"Are you giving me *puppy eyes?*" I asked. Mary Shelley started to scoot closer to the house.

"No way, we aren't going to go in there." There was a NO TRESPASSING sign beside one of the arches, but it was so old and faded that it read N RESPASS G. Mary Shelley whimpered, sticking her nose in the air. That's when I smelled it, too—the same fruity scent that came after the ding-dong-ditcher disappeared. There were tall grasses all around and the lighthouse seemed small and far away. I couldn't help feeling that it wasn't just me and my dog out there.

"Mary Shelley, vamos. *Now,*" I commanded, using my "stern" voice. It usually worked. Most times when she heard that voice, Mary Shelley tucked her tail between her legs and did whatever I asked. This time, though, she ignored me. She gave a big jump and my hand slipped from her collar. "Come back!" I shouted, but she bounded off through the nearest arch and open doorway and disappeared into the building.

I was terrified, but I couldn't just leave my dog to . . . whatever *or whoever* might be in there. "Mary Shelley!" I shouted, running in after her. I pushed the door open a bit and it creaked and groaned. Inside, it was hot, muggy, and smelly. "Mary Shelley," I whispered, but I couldn't hear or see her anymore.

The ground beneath my feet was suddenly harder, and I realized that there was only a thin layer of sand covering what looked like a tile floor. I brushed the sand away to uncover black and white squares. I looked up. The walls were covered in wallpaper that had originally been green, or maybe it had turned that color thanks to the mold. The place smelled terrible—rotten and fishy. Above my head, a single bulb dangled on a thick black wire. To my left, a staircase led upstairs, and there were doorways everywhere I looked.

I heard Mary Shelley growl from beyond one of the doors. Heading her way, I stopped and picked up a branch lying on the floor. It was covered in lichen, but it was sturdy. Back in kindergarten, my parents put me in Little League so I could make some friends, who I eventually had to say goodbye to. I did learn how to swing a stick, though, even if my team nickname had been "Strikeout Kid."

A narrow hallway led to what looked like an old kitchen. Green wallpaper covered this room too. It was peeling everywhere, like a tourist with a bad sunburn.

This place made the lighthouse look really, really good.

Mary Shelley was standing in the middle of the kitchen, snuffling the ground. There was sand everywhere and I guessed that at some point, the place had flooded. That probably accounted for the fishy smell, too.

The cabinets were nearly falling off the walls and all the

doors hung open on rusting hinges. Except for one that was low to the ground and shut tight. *Curiosity killed the cat,* I thought even as I approached the closed cupboard. It was probably empty, like all the other ones, hanging there like open mouths. But what if it wasn't? What if there was something super cool inside? The scientist in me couldn't let a discovery go undiscovered, could I?

Trembling, I reached out for the brass knob. It was cold and slick. "Here goes nothing," I said, and tugged. The door popped open. I knelt down to peer inside.

"Ahhh!" I shouted as a pair of beady eyes looked back at me. I scrambled backward on my butt while Mary Shelley whimpered beside me. I thought it was a raccoon at first, and my brain could only come up with one word—rabies!—while my heart tried to beat out of my chest.

But then I realized the eyes weren't moving. Were they eyes at all? Crawling on all fours, I drew closer until I was face-to-face with the thing in the cabinet.

It was a doll! The creepiest doll ever!

It wore a sailor suit and there was a name stitched into the collar—Bernard. Its face was a little faded and it had black buttons for eyes. Around his neck was a blue thread, and hanging from it was an old-fashioned skeleton key. Slowly, I pulled Bernard out by its foot to get a better look at the face. It didn't look creepy. If anything, it looked sad.

A cool breeze ruffled the top of my head and I dropped Bernard onto the sand, startled. "Just a draft," I told myself, patting down my hair. Mary Shelley sniffed the doll, then she picked it up, soaking it in slobber.

"Ew," I said. "You know, it's probably moldy, like everything else on this island." But Mary Shelley didn't seem to mind. Instead she sat down with Bernard and cuddled it. I checked the rest of the cabinets, just in case there were more cool finds, but they were empty except for spiders and dead beetles.

That's when Mary Shelley whined again. I came over to where she was standing, Bernard still in her jaws.

"That's enough exploring, girl," I said. Then I noticed the floor and I froze.

Someone had written a note by running their fingers through the sand.

HELP ME, FARNK

My first thought was: *AAAAAAhhhh!*

My second thought was: *Whoever wrote that note, they didn't even spell my name right! I mean, Farnk? C'mon.*

And my third thought? *Somebody is playing a trick on me.*

But who? My parents weren't the practical joke type, and there was nobody else around. Unless, of course, we were wrong about that. And if there *was* somebody else on the island, playing ding-dong-ditch and writing my name on the floor of sandy kitchens, then I wasn't sure I wanted to know them at all.

This time, I didn't have to convince Mary Shelley to run. The two of us backed out of the kitchen where my name had been written in the sand and bolted out of the building.

By the time Mary Shelley and I got back to the lighthouse, we were both panting and hot. The whole way, that soft, sweet scent followed us.

"Go away," I whispered at nothing before slamming the door.

"Frankie? You home, mister?" my mom called from somewhere in the lighthouse. She sounded frantic, and alarm bells went off in my brain.

"Mom? You okay?" I called back, undid Mary Shelley's collar, and hung it by the door. She loped away from me, but not before giving me a look that said *Can you believe what just happened?*

I nearly answered my dog's silent question when I heard my mom let out a scream that was followed by a few curse words from my papi. They came running down the stairs together. Mom held a flyswatter in one hand, while Papi seemed to be covered in . . . crabs?

"¡Corre, muchacho!" Papi yelled at me.

"It's an invasion!" Mom shouted.

I held on to the scruff of Mary Shelley's neck and led her out the door. Mom, Papi, Mary Shelley, and I tumbled onto the front walkway and scrambled up the path away from the lighthouse. Papi cursed some more while he plucked blue crabs off his clothes and fingers. Mom helped him, and she did some cursing, too. "Mind your ears, Frankie," she said in between some colorful words.

Mary Shelley and I turned to look at the lighthouse. The front door was open and now I could see them—hundreds of blue crabs crawling down the stairs like they owned the place, their claws clacking in the air.

We'd been forced out of our own home by an army of crustaceans!

"Now what?" Mom asked Papi.

Papi was wiggling his pinched fingers back and forth as he watched the crabs exploring the lighthouse. "We call an exterminator, I guess," he said, and started checking out listings on his phone.

"What's that?" Mom demanded, pointing at the doll in Mary Shelley's mouth.

"We found it. Um, in the sand over there," I lied. I didn't want to tell my parents I'd been exploring the abandoned building, the very one they'd told me was too dangerous to play in.

It took an exterminator AND a plumber to sort out the crabby situation at the lighthouse. Somehow, the creatures had found a way into the pipes and had poured out of the toilet, causing chaos and making the bathroom unusable.

I stood outside with Mary Shelley and my parents as the exterminator and plumber went to work. Outside, the fruity smell lingered, and whenever the breeze kicked up, Mary Shelley would whine.

"Can you smell that?" I asked my mom.

Mom sniffed the air. "Just the ocean, Frankie. Is that what you mean?"

"I smell a big bill," Papi said, narrowing his eyes at the people working on the lighthouse.

Maybe I'd imagined the strange scent. Maybe . . . I sniffed my armpits to make sure. Nope, just the same old Frank aroma. From where we stood, I couldn't see the stone house.

"Hey, Papi," I said, "have you been to that old house on the other end of the key yet?"

"No. It's unsafe to visit," Papi said. "But the views are great on that end of the key. Maybe someday—"

"Don't get ideas, you," Mom said, and Papi rolled his eyes at her like a moody teenager. "Technically, we own it, too, since we bought all the buildings on the key from the county. But the Realtor wouldn't even show it to us because she was *afraid* of the place. Explain that to me, huh?"

"I'm tired of explaining things," Papi said.

I thought about the message in the sand. Maybe whoever was playing a prank out there had been doing it for a long time. Long enough, at least, to scare off potential buyers.

"Well, I'm tired of everything on this island going to pot!" Mom said with a huff.

And *I* was tired of my parents' bickering.

Thankfully they were interrupted by the exterminator,

who had brought some catch-and-release traps for the crabs. He gave all the crabs names as he herded them into traps. "Come on, Julio. Ándale pues, Chico. Let's go, Alfredo." We all laughed at that and for the moment, at least, my parents seemed to forget their argument.

Eventually, the plumber emerged with a frown on his face. "You folks better find somewhere to spend the night."

Mom groaned and immediately started to look for nearby hotels on her cell phone.

"Does this kind of thing happen often?" Papi asked.

The plumber sucked his teeth and looked off into the distance before responding. "Nope. But nothing that happens on Spectacle Key is a surprise," he said, then off he went, back into the lighthouse, tapping a wrench against his hip.

"What's that supposed to mean?" I asked.

"This dang place is cursed, is what it means," I heard my mom say under her breath, and part of me wanted to agree with her.

But cursed? An actual curse? I wondered. Scientists didn't believe in curses. Scientists observed, questioned, hypothesized, experimented, collected data, and came up with conclusions. When it came to living on the island, I was still very much at the beginning of the scientific method. My observation?

Something was very wrong on Spectacle Key.

Chapter 6

GAZING OUT THE WINDOW

We spent the night at a motel on Panther Key, one key over. The room was dingy, and Mary Shelley found a petrified fried shrimp under one of the beds that Mom pried out of her mouth. Mary Shelley exchanged the shrimp for Bernard, her new favorite toy. It thundered all night, but at least we weren't on Spectacle Key.

Morning came soon enough. I packed Bernard up in my overnight suitcase, dumping my dirty pj's and clothes on top of the doll. The plumber called with the all clear, and we drove back to Spectacle Key. As we pulled up the long driveway, I saw a tall woman standing next to a kid my age. He had bright red hair and was wearing a loud green T-shirt with video game characters on it. The woman held a clipboard while the kid fiddled with our mailbox, which was in the shape of a manatee. The mouth opened and closed to reveal a space for mail and he was busy making the manatee "talk."

"Of all the gosh darn people in the ding dang Keys," Mom muttered when she noticed them.

"Be nice, Joyce," Papi said, and put the car in park. "Get your suitcase, Frank," he told me.

The woman with the clipboard had her blond hair tied up in a tight ponytail. She looked familiar, but I couldn't quite place her. The boy who was with her looked up from the manatee mailbox and waved.

"Ms. Shiverton," Mom said, extending her hand for a shake. "What brings you around?"

The Flippy lady!

Emily Shiverton wore a badge with the initials HAUNT beneath her name. It was hot out, but she was wearing a red blazer. A line of sweat trickled down her temple. Emily Shiverton did not shake my mother's hand.

"I understand work has been done to the historical lighthouse recently?" she asked.

"Sí," Papi answered. "We had a crab invasion that took out the plumbing."

Ms. Shiverton smiled. "Did you pull permits for this work?"

"There was no time. It was an emergency," my mom said. The grown-ups continued talking about permits, and city hall, and renovations, but I was distracted by the boy, who was edging closer and closer to Mary Shelley.

"What type of horse is this?" he joked. Mary Shelley was half his height.

"Great Dane," I sighed.

"I know, just playing," the boy said. "I'm eleven. How about you?"

"I'm eleven, too."

The boy gently patted Mary Shelley's head. "It's pretty cool that you live in the lighthouse."

"I think so. Except the place is sort of . . ." I struggled to find the words. "Broken," I settled on saying at last.

He smooshed Mary Shelley's cheeks, and she closed her eyes happily. The boy's hands were covered in Mary Shelley's drool, but he just wiped them on his shirt and kept talking. "Well, do you play Fortcraft? 'Cause I do and maybe we can play online together."

I didn't like video games. My fingers never seemed to cooperate. "I like books. Do you?"

The kid made a face, like I'd just offered him Brussels sprouts for dessert. "Oh," he said. He looked to his mom, who was scribbling on a page in her clipboard and scowling. "No video games, huh?"

"Nope, sorry," I said.

He knelt and picked up a piece of glass. There was junk all around the lighthouse, as if trash was drawn to the place like a magnet. He peered through the glass at me, then used it to draw in the sand at his feet. I watched carefully as he made loops and squiggles, and finally started to write his own name.

His handwriting was awful. *Farnk*, I remembered. Was this kid's penmanship similar to the writing on the sand back at the abandoned building? Was he a terrible speller? Could he be the one who left the note?

I squinted and moved closer, but he erased his name with his foot.

"Hey, what's your name?" he asked.

"As if you don't already know," I said, testing him.

"You're weird." He dropped the shard of glass and went back to the mailbox. "I'm Lucas, by the way."

"I'm Frank," I said. "I've seen your mom on a billboard."

Lucas rolled his eyes. "Oh yeah, the Flippy Award. It's a big deal to her, but it's kind of embarrassing."

Honestly, I'd be embarrassed, too. But just because we had that in common didn't mean I could trust him. I wasn't about to let some kid play tricks on me just when I'd moved to a new place. Not a chance!

"Why is it called a Flippy Award anyway?"

This time, Lucas rolled his eyes so far that I thought he might be able to see out the back of his head. "Because the award is shaped like a dolphin. It's a bronze dolphin about this big." He gestured with his hands, suggesting a shape the length of a ruler. "And my mom wants it more than anything in the world. Our whole family has lived in the Keys for generations. My mom says it's about time a Shiverton wins."

"I hope she does, then," I said truthfully.

Lucas shrugged. "Yeah, right. My mom said that you and your family have 'put a wrench in her plans,' whatever that means."

"That doesn't make any sense. We just live here."

Lucas answered with another shrug. It seemed to be his favorite method of communication. When I asked him what school was like, he did it again, so I abandoned the conversation. Without saying another word, I left Lucas, his mom, and my parents in the driveway to talk about whatever it was they all needed to discuss. "Come on, Mary Shelley," I said, but when she didn't follow me into the lighthouse, I turned around and saw that Lucas was smooshing her face again, and Mary Shelley was thumping her tail so hard into the sand that I thought she might break through to sea level.

"Traitor," I whispered at my dog, then went inside.

Back in the lighthouse, the crabs were gone and, thankfully, the toilet was in working condition again. But when Mom tried to light the gas stove to make dinner, the pilot light wouldn't come on.

"Dang it all!" she roared. Papi and I came running into the kitchen.

"Don't tell me—" Papi started.

Mom just pointed at the stove in silence. Her mouth was a grim, tight line and her nostrils flared. "I hate this place. Hate."

"Home, remember? And your father is nearby now, too," Papi said.

My mom sighed and pushed back her hair. "Just frustrated, that's all."

"We can just microwave something for dinner tonight." Papi patted her shoulder and spoke in a soft voice, nice and slow, which I think only made Mom angry again.

"Please don't speak to me like a child," she said.

"Hey!" I protested. Any insult to children was personal. But my parents didn't even notice that I'd said anything. While they argued, Papi poured himself a cup of cold coffee. He slid it into the microwave, which he'd purchased back in Auburn before the move, slammed the door, punched in the time, and hit start.

Mom was leaning on the counter, her hand over her face. "When are you going to realize this was a mistake?"

Papi paced the kitchen, ruffling his own hair with both hands, which he always did when he was nervous. "Mistake? This home has potential!"

I agreed with both of them. Everything was going wrong, just like Mom said it would. The stove wouldn't be the last problem, I knew. But Papi had a point, too. The lighthouse, when fixed, could be really awesome to live in! It was unique, and we had the island all to ourselves. Plus, it was built to last, so we didn't have to worry about hurricanes. Even better? If it worked out, we wouldn't have to move again.

A strange smell interrupted my thoughts. It was metallic, like that gross, pukey scent that comes out of toolboxes that have been closed for a long time. Mary Shelley, who never missed an opportunity to visit the kitchen when people were in it, hoping that one of us would drop some food by accident, whimpered and sourced the smell. Her big nose pointed right to the microwave.

Oh no, I thought as I turned to see smoke pouring out of the brand-new machine. I ran over just as Mom and Papi noticed it, too. Mom unplugged the microwave. "This place is cursed!" she shouted before storming out, leaving me, Papi, and Mary Shelley in the kitchen.

"I'll order takeout," Papi muttered.

"Cursed," I said to Mary Shelley, who whimpered again. "Don't worry, girl," I tried to assure her as I poured kibble into her bowl. Mary Shelley chomped down on it quickly, leaving me to my thoughts.

Then I remembered—curses weren't real. What was real were facts. And evidence. The electrical wiring in the kitchen was probably bad, which was why the stove and microwave broke. The crab invasion probably had something to do with changes in the shoreline. As for the lighthouse lamp? It was ancient. Of course it wouldn't work after all this time! How could I show my parents that they were getting worked up over completely logical events?

I climbed the stairs to my bedroom and an idea came to mind—I'd write a proof! Ms. McCartney had taught us how to do them. A proof is an argument for a math or science problem, written down, stating facts that lead to the correct conclusion.

The lighthouse was *not* cursed. That was what I would set out to prove. I would show my excellently argued proof to my parents, and maybe then they'd stop fighting and start working together.

There's nothing like a plan to make me feel a lot better, so I was practically floating up the stairs, already building the proof in my head. But when I opened my bedroom door, I stopped in my tracks. Everything was as it should be. There were no crabs crawling on the walls. My alarm clock hadn't exploded. My bed was unmade, like it always was, and my suitcase, which I'd opened but hadn't unpacked yet, was still stuffed with my clothes.

Except.

Bernard wasn't under my dirty shirts and shorts.

Bernard was sitting on the windowsill, staring out over Spectacle Key.

The proof that had materialized in my head on the way up the stairs disappeared in an imaginary cloud of dust.

I sat on the other side of my room, staring at Bernard, who stared out the window. I was trying to come up with an explanation for why the doll had escaped my suitcase, but nothing stuck. Mom and Papi hadn't come up to the third floor since we'd gotten home from Panther Key. I'd been unzipping my suitcase when I heard Mom shouting about the stove. And unless I was blanking on it, I hadn't put a hand on Bernard.

Just then Mary Shelley came lumbering into my room.

She went straight for the doll, opened her mouth, and grabbed it by the waist, then settled down to cuddle it.

I snapped my fingers. It must have been Mary Shelley!

"Hey, girl, gimme that," I said, and Mary Shelley reluctantly opened her mouth. Bernard was covered in slobber, which I wiped off on the rug. "Gross, but not cursed," I said to the doll, as if it could hear me. I tossed Bernard on my bed. Mary Shelley stood up, aiming to retrieve what she now considered her toy. "Stay," I said, and she did, settling back down and giving me a resentful look.

Feeling a bit better, I finished unpacking my things and then started building the proof in my head again. I got out my notebook and pen and started putting the proof together.

PROOF

Proving That Both Mom and Papi Are Right About the Lighthouse and Should, Therefore, Stop Fighting

ABSTRACT

Logical thinking explains nearly every phenomenon that a person might wonder about. This proof will argue that the problems with the lighthouse are not due to a curse. The lighthouse's age and disrepair are the causes of the problems being experienced today.

This proof will also argue that it really is hard to live in a place like this. Frustrations are normal and all feelings should be respected.

Hence, Mom and Papi are BOTH RIGHT and should STOP FIGHTING.

I was feeling really proud of what I'd come up with so far and was about to start listing my evidence when Mary Shelley barked twice. I looked up to where she was sitting, panting and pointing her nose at Bernard, who was back on the windowsill, staring out.

"Come on, girl," I groaned. "Quit playing." I yanked Bernard off the sill by his arm and tossed him onto the top shelf in my closet, where even Mary Shelley couldn't reach. Mary Shelley whined, then sniffed her butt before settling back down again.

I was halfway through writing my proof when Papi called up the stairs. "I've got some ropa vieja with your name on it, Frank! ¡Dale!"

"Yes!" I shouted. Cuban takeout was my favorite, and we hadn't had any since we'd moved to the lighthouse. I barreled down the steps and Mary Shelley loped behind me. Mom and Papi were sitting at the dining table, serving themselves plates of steaming deliciousness. I piled platanitos, moros, and ropa vieja onto my plate.

Mom was chewing thoughtfully and Papi was shoveling food into his mouth like it was about to disappear. Nobody said a word. Everything felt . . . tense. The faucet drip, drip, dripped while we ate, and with each drop of water, Papi's left eye twitched. Overhead, the kitchen light made a steady hissing sound. Every once in a while, the ice maker in the refrigerator rattled. We all watched as a lizard crawled up the wall, slipping into a crack in the mortar. It got stuck halfway through, and when it finally disappeared, it left behind its tail, which fell to the floor and twitched pathetically for a while.

Surprisingly, none of us said a word about the lizard's tail. We just kept on eating dinner. Maybe we were getting used to this crazy place. That's when a knock on the door made Mom jump out of her seat.

"Now what?" She sighed and got up to see who was at the door. She was only gone a minute when she returned with a package in her hands. "It's for you, Frankie. From Pop-Pop!"

The box was dinged on one side, but Pop-Pop had wrapped it in so much tape that I was sure the contents were safe. I tore it open with a grunt. A chemistry set!

Now don't go trying to build any monsters out of spare parts, you hear? he'd written on a note fixed to the set.

Carefully I unpacked glass test tubes, flasks, and pipettes right there on the kitchen table. There was a petri dish for growing mold, litmus paper to test acids, a plastic periodic table, and a glossy pamphlet describing projects I could do with everything. At the bottom of the box was a tattered book from 1963 titled *Experiments for Young Scientists*, Pop-Pop's old lab goggles, a handful of vials, and an actual Bunsen burner.

"I don't know about all this stuff," Mom said. "My father seems to forget you're only eleven."

"Let's stick to the nonflammable experiments for now, okay?" Papi added.

I kept my mouth shut. Inside one of the test tubes was a rolled-up piece of paper, which I opened when Mom and Papi weren't looking. On the page, Pop-Pop had written: *You can do some real science with this stuff. Just make sure to wash your hands, shield your eyes, and don't burn down the house. Also: don't tell your folks.*

Okay, Pop-Pop, I thought, trying to hold in a laugh.

"Can I be excused?" I asked. I pointed at my plate. "President of the Clean Plate Club here."

"Go on, mister," Mom said.

I put the pieces of the chemistry set back in the box along with the book and goggles, then climbed the stairs to my bedroom. Mary Shelley climbed up after me. I planned on working on my proof some more, then settling down to read about experiments I could do.

But when I got to my room, I stopped in my tracks. Mary Shelley slammed into my back, nearly knocking me over. There, on the windowsill, was Bernard again, looking out toward the abandoned building.

Directly in front of Bernard, somebody had run their finger through the dirt on the exterior of the window, twenty feet in the air, and written two words:

FARNK? HELP?

Chapter 7

AN EXPERIMENT GOES WRONG

Here's the thing: there was no way—*no way*—that a possessed doll had written those words on the outside of my window. Also? I didn't think for a single second that Bernard had marched himself off the top shelf in my closet and sat on the windowsill all on his own.

So there was only one possibility.

Someone was playing a joke on me.

It's not like people hadn't ever messed with me before. Back in second grade, when we were living in a converted school bus in Portland, Anna James hid my lunch in different locations every day for a week. She didn't get caught until Monday's bologna sandwich began to reek inside the teacher's desk. And in fourth grade, Michael Padron stuck gum in my hair while we played heads up, seven up. We'd been living in a grain silo in Texas then.

This was just another dumb joke. And if I had to guess who was doing it, a certain redheaded gamer and his clipboard-toting mother came to mind. Lucas and HAUNT. They were my only suspects, and who could blame me? From the looks of it, Ms. Emily Shiverton's number-one goal was to pester my parents about the lighthouse. Plus, her group was named *HAUNT.* How creepy was that? She was hiding in plain sight! I couldn't figure out how they'd gotten in, though. Maybe Lucas had snuck in through the back door while we were having dinner. I'd check the locks for evidence of picking later.

As for the window, a tall ladder would do the trick. Or maybe somebody used a very, very long stick to smudge the letters into the dirt.

It was Lucas, his mom, and HAUNT. It had to be.

"We one hundred percent will figure this one out on our own, Mary Shelley," I said to my dog, who cocked her head at me and blinked slowly. "No need to bother Mom and Papi with it." I could hear my parents arguing downstairs about something now that I'd left them alone. They had enough to worry about.

I grabbed Bernard and tossed him to Mary Shelley, who plucked him out of the air with a chomp and then settled down for some not-so-haunted doll snuggles.

Next I looked through the chemistry set Pop-Pop had sent me. Maybe there was something here that could help with my investigation. I set aside beakers and pipettes, a fistful of cork stoppers, some dry chemicals in little packets, litmus paper, an instruction book, and yes! There it was! A fingerprint detection kit in a cardboard box!

I glanced back at the words written on the window. *Farnk,* I thought grumpily. I remembered how Lucas had used a piece of glass to write in the sand. While I couldn't match the handwriting there to the one on the window and back at the ruin, the glass would tell the story of his fingerprints.

Rushing down the stairs and out through the front door, I scanned the ground for the glass Lucas had used to scribble in the sand. The sun was striking it so that it glittered where he'd dropped it. "Success!" I said to myself, and pocketed the shard. Back up the stairs I went, past my glowering parents, who were now staring at each other across the kitchen table without blinking, and I climbed and climbed until I was back in my bedroom.

Of course, there was Mary Shelley at the foot of my bed, fast asleep, and Bernard was keeping watch at the window. This time, I left him there. If Mary Shelley wanted to keep her toy on the sill, it was fine with me.

The fingerprint detection kit included dusting powder in a little bag, tape for "lifting" fingerprints off surfaces, a magnifying glass, and a little feather brush to sweep away the dust. I worked carefully and was able to get Lucas's fingerprints off the piece of glass. I'd have to return to the ruin to see if I could get any more prints there. And once I found a match, voilà! Lucas would be so busted.

* * *

In the morning, I ate my breakfast cereal in four big spoonfuls.

"What's the rush, Frankie?" Mom asked. She had her hair tied up in a yellow scarf and was scrubbing the oven with some stinky spray.

"Gonna play with Pop-Pop's chemistry set outside before it gets too hot."

"Good idea. When I was a little girl, your pop-pop always came home from the lab smelling like fire and brimstone. Best keep it outdoors," she said, then coughed through a fog of oven cleaner.

I shoved all the parts of the chemistry set into a duffel bag, adding the magnifying glass Ms. McCartney had given me. Then I left the lighthouse with Mary Shelley. She bounded out into the sunshine, snapping at butterflies and missing them on purpose. Soon we reached the old building. I stopped in its shadow.

Okay, I told myself. *Nothing strange is happening here. It's just a prank.*

I squared my shoulders and stepped inside. The wind had swept some more of the sand off the floor, and I could see a red-and-green-tile pattern everywhere. A giant bookcase took up one entire back wall, but the shelves were saggy and there wasn't a book to be found. Off to the left was the kitchen where I'd seen my name misspelled in the sand. That was where I had to start.

Quietly, I stepped into the kitchen. There it was—FARNK—written in the sand. Mary Shelley wandered around, leaving huge paw prints everywhere and whining every so often.

"I know, girl," I said. "This place gives me the creeps, too."

Settling down in a corner of the kitchen, I removed the fingerprint detection kit from my duffel bag. I walked around the kitchen, trying to imagine what the prankster might have touched. The problem was, everything was *already* dusty or sand covered. I peered through the magnifying glass but didn't see any disturbed surfaces. I'd never get a print off anything here!

Eventually I gave up. "This is useless," I said out loud, and put away the fingerprint stuff. I'd have to find some other way to bust Lucas. Inside the duffel, the vials full of powders and chemicals rattled. "I might as well have some fun while we're here, right?" I told Mary Shelley, who looked doubtful. The more time I spent in the abandoned house, the surer I was that there was absolutely nothing scary about the place. I'd just let my imagination run away with me that first time.

I flipped through the book Pop-Pop had packed with the set. There were experiments to make something called "elephant toothpaste," the usual baking-soda-and-vinegar foam explosions, litmus paper tests, even how to make a levitating magnet! But the experiment that caught my eye was one on exothermic reactions, which are reactions that give off lots of cool light and heat. It would be like my own fireworks show!

There was no way Mom or Papi would let me try one of those. Mom would say something like, "Safety first, mister," and Papi would make up a story about a kid back in Cuba who burned down his whole neighborhood. Some experiments were best kept secret. After all, did Dr. Frankenstein tell his parents about his monster creation? Nope, he just kept it all nice and quiet in his laboratory. I didn't have a lab, but an abandoned building would be the PERFECT place for my experiment.

I set everything up in the center of the kitchen, brushing aside my misspelled name. *Take that, jokester!* Mary Shelley curled up by the back door and was soon snoring. I put a test tube in its stand and poured in a bit of potassium chlorate from a labeled bag. Using a dropper, I squeezed a few drops of sulfuric acid into the test tube. I heard a small hissing sound and remembered the goggles.

"Sorry, Pop-Pop!" I said, imagining him standing there, scowling at me for not following safety rules. I secured the goggles over my eyes, wiping dust off them. Then I went back to the instructions in the book. *Add ¼ teaspoon of sugar.* I dove into the duffel bag but didn't find any sugar. That's when I heard Mary Shelley smacking her tongue around her mouth. An empty sugar packet fluttered across the floor.

"You're lucky that was only sugar, dog," I said, even though my heart was pounding. There were lots of dangerous and poisonous things in the set that Mary Shelley might have eaten instead. Just in case, I zipped the bag closed. *Better remember to do that from now on,* I told myself.

Without sugar as an activator, the test tube just sat there, sad and boring.

That's when I remembered that Frank Fernández always has a nutritional supplement in his pocket, also known as leftover candy. I shoved my hand into my pocket and pulled out a few gummy bears. They were Pop-Pop's favorite and mine, too. Gummy bears were so chewy and good—and most importantly, sugary!

I chose a red one and dropped it into the test tube.

Immediately, the hissing grew louder, and with a pop, a blast of red fire erupted from the top of the tube! "Success!" I shouted, and waited for the fire to fizzle back into the tube and die out. That's how these experiments usually went. Like those volcanoes kids make for science class, they were only exciting for a few seconds.

But the fire only grew redder, the flame burning hotter and longer, until it was nearly reaching the ceiling. It looked like a long, slithery tongue that seemed to lick the air around it.

Oh no. This was very bad.

"Mary Shelley, we have to go!" I yelled, but my dog snored on. I ran to her and tugged on her collar, but an 80-pound Great Dane is not easily moved, especially when they're asleep. She was in a sugar-induced power nap!

The fire crackled. Beneath that sound I started to hear something else—the cries of little kids and a howling wind, even though the skies were clear and blue. "Is anybody there?" I shouted, but then the noises died away. Maybe I'd imagined them. The fire grew taller and my armpits started sweating. We needed to leave!

I climbed on top of Mary Shelley, lifted her ear, and screamed into it, "WAKE UP!"

My dog blinked her eyes open and licked me from chin to forehead. But just as she got to her feet at last and I turned to bolt, the fire disappeared. The test tube was empty. All around, written in the sand, was my name.

FARNKFARNKFARNKFARNK FARNK
FARNKFARNKFARNKFARNKFARNK

And standing beside the experiment was a white girl in a short brown dress and an apron, her light brown hair in two braids, and freckles all over her nose and cheeks.

"How do you do?" she asked.

Instead of answering, I screamed my head off.

Chapter 8

A GIRL WITHOUT A NAME

The girl clamped her hands over her ears when I started yelling. I stumbled backward, tripping over Mary Shelley and flopping onto my back. As I lay there, the girl bent to hover over me.

"Please don't scream again, Farnk."

"My name is not FARNK!" I shouted. She covered her ears again. "Sorry," I added. "It's Frank."

The girl turned in a circle, eyeing my name in the sand all around us. "It isn't? Then why do you spell it like that?"

"YOU spelled it like that!"

The girl looked suddenly offended. "I did *not*. I'll have you know that I always received top marks in spelling *and* penmanship, and this handwriting is atrocious."

That stumped me. Hadn't she written my name in the

sand? "I thought you did it," I said.

"Why would I do something like this?" she asked.

I sat up but held on tight to Mary Shelley. "You tell me. Why does anything happen on this weird island?"

The girl sat, too, and laid her hand on Mary Shelley's giant paw. "Indeed. That's a very good question. It's a strange place."

"You can say that again," I said.

"It's a strange place," the girl repeated.

"I didn't mean that literally."

"Oh."

Mary Shelley rested her head on the girl's lap, drooling a puddle into her skirt, but the girl didn't seem to mind. I assumed she was from one of the nearby keys and had walked over a connecting bridge to get here.

"Spectacle Key really is weird, though. We had a crab invasion this week. What's it like on your key?" I asked, purposely avoiding the subjects of possessed dolls, HAUNT, and bickering parents.

The girl's eyes got a faraway look in them, as if she were remembering something painful. "It's hard to explain," she said at last.

My fear was going away, bit by bit. The girl's freckles covered every inch of her face. I liked them. They reminded me of Mary Shelley's soft belly, which was also full of freckles. I couldn't explain it, but I believed her when she said she wasn't playing a prank on me.

"So where do you live? Little Boat Key, or Panther Key maybe? How long did it take you to walk here, anyway?"

She gulped and her eyes filled with tears. "I don't know," she whimpered. "All I know is that it was very dark, and then there was a spark of light, and now I'm here. This place is like a memory from a long time ago."

"A dark place?" I repeated. Had she been trapped in one of the rooms in the old building and fallen asleep? Did the sounds from the experiment wake her up? Maybe she hit her head and didn't remember how she got there.

The girl nodded. "Frank, are you meant to help me?"

"Are you lost?" I asked.

"I think so," she said.

A chill ran up and down my body, like an electric current. My biggest fear when I was little was getting lost. I used to hold on to my mom's and papi's hands everywhere we went. "Okay then. No wonder you're scared. What's your name?"

The girl shook her head.

"Come on, you can tell me," I said. Mary Shelley licked the girl's hands in agreement.

"I don't remember!" she wailed, slumping over Mary Shelley and sobbing.

Panic made me break into a sweat. I never, ever knew how to react when someone cried. Should I say "there, there," or "I'm sorry," or nothing at all? But my parents were great at comforting me when I was little and used to cry all the time. "My mom and papi will know what to do," I said, unsure whether to pat her shoulder, so I didn't touch her. "If you follow me to the lighthouse where I live, my parents can help. I promise."

The girl raised her head, wiping fat tears off her cheeks with the heel of her hand. Silently, I stood up and packed the chemistry set back into the duffel bag. She stood right beside me the whole time, like a shadow. It was a little bit unnerving. I wondered if she had amnesia and whether that was why she didn't remember her own name.

And I thought *I* didn't have a friend in the world besides Mary Shelley. Things on Spectacle Key got weirder by the moment—and this girl topped them all!

"Follow me," I said. "My folks can help," I repeated again and again as we walked through the abandoned building. She stopped at the arched doorway.

"Frank, this all feels very familiar."

"The island?" I asked. Ahead of us, the sun was baking the sand and tall grasses, and dozens of dragonflies perched on the slender green blades, balancing almost as if by magic.

"Mm-hmm," she said, squinting at the sunshine. "Can I hold your hand?" she asked out of the blue.

I'd never held a girl's hand before. Her fingers were stretched out toward me, small and thin. "Okay," I said, and stuck out my palm. My knees were a little shaky, and I didn't know if it was because of the scary fire, the mysterious girl, or the hand-holding.

She put her warm hand in mine. She seemed braver than

before, so I guess it was worth it.

We tromped through the grass. Mary Shelley led the way, and every once in a while she would bound back as if making sure we were following. A thought struck me then: I'd hardly ever spent time with another kid outside of school. Sure, this girl had appeared under very strange circumstances, but she was kind of nice. Maybe, once we figured out where she came from, we could hang out.

But she had grown very quiet as we walked, and I started to get nervous about the silence.

"I saw a dolphin the other day," I blurted. I wasn't sure how to start a conversation. Being Friendless Frank and all, I didn't have much practice. But I figured dolphins had to be cool enough to get her talking.

"Did you? Really?" she asked excitedly.

Before I could answer, she wrenched me toward the beach. Grasses whipped the sides of our faces as we ran, and a burrowing owl zoomed out of a stand of sea grapes. When we stopped at last, we were right at the edge of the water. Waves touched the tips of her brown boots and wet my toes. Mary Shelley darted in and out of the ocean, snapping at the foam.

"How do you spot them?" she asked eagerly.

I squinted my eyes. The ocean was as flat as a plate. "It should be easy today. Look for a fin."

The girl concentrated on the water. I realized I was still holding her hand then, so I let go, hoping that wasn't rude. It seemed like a good time to ask her more questions. "You don't remember anything about where you came from?" I asked as she stared out at the horizon.

She shook her head.

"Maybe try retracing your steps," I suggested. "What's the last thing you remember?"

The girl squeezed her eyes very tightly and held her breath. Her nose got all wrinkly, and she tightened her grip on my hand. "Rain. Scary rain."

"That's not so helpful. It rains here a lot," I said.

"No, I suppose it's n—" she started to say, but stopped and pointed to a spot in the distance. "Dolphin!" she yelled, and gave me the biggest smile. There it was—a dorsal fin slicing through the water about twenty feet away.

Mary Shelley barked at the sea. The dolphin jumped out of the water and splashed back in smoothly.

"Amazing, right?" I asked.

"Dolphins sure are swell," she replied.

"Um. Yeah. What you said." The sun made the water sparkle. A pair of seagulls twirled in the sky around one another. Spectacle Key was weird and a little bit creepy a lot of the time.

But sometimes?

It was magical.

"We should go see my parents," I suggested, and the girl agreed.

We walked on for a bit, leaving the sea at our backs. The lighthouse loomed before us, larger as we got closer. "You live inside the actual lighthouse?" the girl asked. "Don't these things usually have a keeper's cottage attached?"

"Good eye," I said, which was what Pop-Pop always told me when I noticed something important. "The keeper's cottage was destroyed in a mega-hurricane a long time ago. Past owners converted the inside of the lighthouse itself into useful rooms."

"I don't like storms," the girl said.

"Me neither." Living all over, I'd experienced tornadoes, nor'easters, and blizzards. But I hadn't ever lived through a hurricane. Mom and Papi had stories to tell about hurricanes like Andrew, Katrina, and Maria, and I hoped never to have a storm story to match theirs.

Undoing the latch to the front door, I was immediately greeted by the sounds of my parents' latest argument.

"I'm telling you the durn toilets aren't flushing the right way! The water is supposed to swirl clockwise in this hemisphere. Haven't you heard of the Coriolis effect? We don't live in Australia, so why's the toilet water swirling the wrong way?" my mom was yelling.

"Who gives tres pepinos how the water flushes, as long as it does?" Papi answered.

The girl and Mary Shelley had followed me all the way to the downstairs half bath where my parents stood yelling at each other about toilet water. I cleared my throat.

"This is the northern hemisphere and this toilet is NOT RIGHT."

I cleared my throat again.

Papi started pushing the button that flushed the toilet again and again. "Who cares?" he asked with each button smash.

"Mom, Papi, my friend needs help. She's in bad trouble," I said. My parents stopped arguing at once. That's the thing about their fights—I always knew that I came first, no matter what.

Mom gripped my shoulders and Papi leaned over a little to hear me better.

"Where is she?" Mom and Papi asked at the same time.

The girl's hand was suddenly in mine again, and she gave my fingers a squeeze.

"Um. Here. Right here. She doesn't remember her name or how she got onto the island. We've got to help," I said.

My parents looked behind me, then they looked at each other. "Where is she, Frank? The kitchen or something?" Papi asked, peering past me into the distance.

"Here!" I said, lifting her hand in mine.

My mom felt my forehead. "You've gone and given yourself heatstroke out there," she said, worry all over her face. "Let's get you something to drink and then you can go lie down."

"Say something," I said to the girl, feeling frantic, thinking that maybe I did give myself heatstroke.

"How do you do?" the girl asked my parents very politely.

"See?" I said.

Now it was Papi's turn to feel my cheeks for a fever. "Either he's gone loopy or he's playing a trick on us."

"That's not very funny, mister," Mom said. "We've got too much going on, like toilets ignoring the magnetic pull of the earth!"

"Not this again!" Papi roared.

I looked at the girl, who shrugged and said, "At least *you* can see me, Frank. That's something. Like I said, this island? It's a strange place."

Chapter 9

ZIRCONIUM

I tried to introduce the girl to my parents again at lunchtime, but they still couldn't see her. *Now what?* I wondered, feeling a bit like Dr. Frankenstein. Once he made his monster, he didn't have a clue what to do with it. A girl who'd lost her memory was believable. She probably had amnesia. An invisible girl, though? There had to be a scientific reason for it. I took my own temperature a few times, but I didn't have a fever, so I didn't think I was hallucinating her. I read once about people having blind spots in their vision. Maybe the girl just happened to be standing in the precise location where my parents couldn't see her. But even that was hard to believe. I was stumped.

As for my parents, Papi muttered something about me being too big to have an imaginary friend. Mom, sensing my frustration, started saying stuff like, "Make yourself at home, Friend of Frank," while facing the wrong direction.

"It's all right, Frank," the girl said.

It was pretty far from all right, but I didn't say that, at least not in front of Mom and Papi. Instead, I refilled my bowl with mac and cheese and asked, "Can I finish this upstairs? I think I did get too much sun after all."

"Sure thing, mister," my mom said, excusing me from the table.

I whispered as I climbed the stairs. "This bowl is for you. I'm sure you're hungry."

"That's curious," the girl said. "I'm not hungry at all."

The last thing I needed was for this invisible girl, which was what I was now calling her in my head, to faint from starvation. "You'd better try, just in case," I said. When we reached my room, I closed the door behind the girl and Mary Shelley so that it was just the three of us again.

The girl stopped at the sight of Bernard, still sitting at the window. "Oh, I don't like that doll at all!"

"I found it in the ruin the other day."

"And today you found me." She shivered all over and rubbed the goose bumps that had appeared on her arms. Slowly, she walked up to Bernard and poked his hat with a trembling finger. The doll pitched forward into the window-pane and the girl jumped back.

"Here, sit and eat, and let me think about your situation for a bit," I said. She plopped onto the rug, crossed her legs, and started picking at the mac and cheese. Mary Shelley whined for a bite and I caught her sneaking my dog a forkful.

I watched while the girl chewed the food. She seemed like a regular kid, except her clothes were old-fashioned. For the first time I noticed her shoes. They were lace-up boots that stopped at her ankles and they were caked in old mud. The laces were a bright red. Who wore boots in Florida? I wiggled my flip-flops. She patted Mary Shelley's head with one hand as she shoveled food into her mouth with the other. I guess she was hungry after all.

After a while, I noticed something else—no matter how much food she seemed to put in her mouth, the bowl never got empty. The mac and cheese looked untouched. I watched more closely. Into her mouth went a forkful of cheesy pasta, out came a clean fork. But the amount of lunch in her bowl remained the same.

"You sure you don't remember anything about who you are and where you came from?" I asked.

She shook her head, her mouth full of food, then swallowed. "Not a thing."

I remembered how we'd had a ding-dong-ditcher at the lighthouse earlier that week.

"Hey, did you knock on the lighthouse door a few days ago?"

She narrowed her eyes at me and frowned. "I've just met you, Frank. Don't you believe me?"

I did. Or at least, I wanted to. I couldn't discount the idea that my parents were in on the trick, that they would burst into my room any minute now, laughing about my "imaginary friend," who happened to be a neighbor one key over. But if that were true, then this girl was a very good actor because her eyes were getting all teary as she waited for me to answer her. "I believe you," I said.

She slumped in relief. "I'm glad." She put down the bowl of mac and cheese and patted her belly. "And I'm stuffed."

Mary Shelley dove in, finishing the food that the girl didn't even seem to have started. But I'd watched her eat it! Could I not even trust my own eyes?

Maybe I really was suffering from heatstroke.

The girl crawled over to the duffel bag with the chemistry set. "May I?" she asked, and I nodded. She unzipped the bag and rummaged through the contents, pulling out a poster that was folded into fourths.

"That's the periodic table," I said when she opened it all the way and laid it out on the rug. "It shows the names of the elements."

"What are elements?"

I thought for a moment, remembering what I'd learned in science last year. "First of all, elements seem invisible, like you. They are made up only of themselves. So, for example, carbon is an element that is only made up of carbon! But Mary Shelley is a dog that's made up of carbon, oxygen, and loads of other elements."

The girl scrunched up her nose at the poster. "Do you

have a favorite element?" she asked.

"No, that would be silly," I said.

She cleared her throat and pursed her lips at me. Obviously, she'd already picked a favorite. She let her finger sit on a big *Zr* on the left side of the poster. "That one. Zirconium. Perhaps that can be my name, since I don't remember it. Zirconium. It has a nice ring to it."

"Um. It's a bit long. My name is long, too. It's Francisco, but everyone calls me Frank."

The girl stood up, straightened her skirt, and held out her hand, as if we were meeting for the first time. "Zirconium can be shortened. I'm Connie, then. Nice to meet you."

I laughed. "We've already met!"

"Not formally. It's best to be polite from the start," she said.

"Okay then, Connie. I'm Frank." I laughed again.

"You have a wonderful laugh, Frank. You should use it more often." Connie laughed herself, closing her eyes and wrinkling her nose.

I could feel myself blushing. "Thanks. You know, I really hope you aren't a symptom of heatstroke, or a figment of my imagination," I said, surprising myself. Connie was kind of cool and hadn't tried to play any tricks on me or made fun of me yet.

"I hope so too," Connie said, then she came and sat on the edge of my bed, looking thoughtful. "Frank, why can't I remember anything about myself? Everything seems so unfamiliar. Like your clothes. I hope I'm not being rude, but where are the buttons on your shirt? Your shoes are very colorful but don't look sturdy. And your mother was wearing trousers. A bit scandalous, don't you think?"

I sat up to stare at my flip-flops and ran a hand over my T-shirt. They seemed all right to me. And Mom always wore jeans!

"Well, your clothes are funny to me," I said. "What's up with those boots?"

The girl crossed her arms. "I'll have you know that this dress . . . this dress . . . was made by . . . um . . . by my . . . um . . . oh, I don't remember!" she cried. "Somebody made it for me, but who? Why can't I remember anything?" The girl crumpled into a ball on my bed, sobbing. Mary Shelley jumped up to help and licked the top of her head until it was a tangled, drool-soaked mess.

If my parents couldn't help, then I *had* to find someone who could. But how would I do that when Connie was invisible? The police would laugh me right out of the station. And if I kept bugging my parents about my "imaginary friend," they'd take me to the hospital for heatstroke treatment.

Back in Auburn, I might have found someone at the university who could help. There had to be some professor who knew all about invisibility. But what resources did I have on the Keys? There were a billion Flippy billboards, a dolphin rescue center, a shop that sold things made out of seashells . . .

That's when I remembered the wooden sign near the entrance to Spectacle Key, the one advertising Mama Z: Mystic and Reader with the words *EYE SEE ALL* beneath her name!

Connie was invisible. We needed somebody who would take her problem seriously. I didn't know Mama Z, but if what she claimed was true, if she really "saw all," then maybe she'd "see" Connie, too. And if she could, then we could work backward from that and try to figure out why Connie was invisible in the first place.

"We'll find out who you really are, Connie, and why your clothes are funny and who made them, I promise," I whispered.

Connie looked up at me with red-rimmed eyes and a drippy nose. "Thank you, Frank. But you're the one in funny clothes."

We both laughed. Then Mary Shelley jumped up on the bed, knocking Connie right off, which made us laugh even harder! That's when my mom opened the door to my room. She was holding a plate with a slice of apple pie on it.

"Glad you're feeling better, mister. Want some pie? I brought two forks, too. One for you and one for your imaginary friend."

"She's not—" I started to say, then added, "Never mind."

Mom nodded like she understood. Then she sat on my bed, nudging Mary Shelley over. "I had a special friend like yours once, back when I was growing up here in the Keys. He was a sad boy who never told me his name."

"How did you know he was sad?" I asked. Connie was watching my mom with wide eyes, tears falling down her cheeks again.

Mom was thoughtful for a moment. "How do you know when anyone is sad? You pay attention. How about you? Is your imaginary friend sad? You told us earlier that she was lost."

"Yeah. Sometimes she's sad," I said, and tried not to look at Connie.

Mom ruffled my hair. "Oh, mister, I know it's been hard moving here. Papi and I are going to make it work for all of us, you'll see. And I know you'll make friends at school in the fall. Maybe you won't feel so lost then." Mom's eyes welled up a little. I didn't bother correcting her.

"I'm okay. Really. What happened to your imaginary friend, Mom?" I asked, changing the subject back to her story.

"He went away at some point. I haven't thought about him in a long time, actually." Mom chewed her thumbnail for a moment, and she suddenly looked very young. "That's how imaginary friends are, I guess." She handed me the slice of pie with the two forks and left my room.

When she was gone, Connie spoke up. "I'm not imaginary, Frank. Also, can I share that pie with you?"

I really hoped she was right. "Dig in," I said. "And afterward, we're going to go see somebody about your problem," I added, thinking about Mama Z and her all-seeing eye.

Chapter 10

MAMA Z

After lunch, I told my parents I was going for a walk around the island. I didn't mention that I would be going to the next key over in search of Mama Z's help. My piggy bank had thirty bucks in it, and I emptied the thing, hoping Mama Z wouldn't charge more than that. It was all I had—saved from birthday and tooth fairy money.

"Take Mary Shelley with you," Papi called.

"And don't forget your imaginary friend," Mom added.

"Don't encourage that," I heard Papi say as I closed the front door, followed by Mom's voice rising in response.

Connie, Mary Shelley, and I walked in silence. It was so hot I could practically feel my skin sizzle. Mary Shelley was panting. I glanced over at Connie's long sleeves. She wasn't sweating at all.

"Your parents bicker a lot," Connie said after a while. It was very windy, and her two braids flipped around like propellers.

"They didn't used to. It's that busted lighthouse. It's so much work and everything is always breaking down."

"I don't know. Something about Spectacle Key seems . . . wrong," Connie said. We were just stepping onto the footpath that ran along the bridge out of the island. Mangroves grew on either side of the bridge, their roots tangled up in shallow, salty water. Bit by bit, the wind died down as we walked until the air was totally still. "See what I mean?" Connie said, turning to look at Spectacle Key behind us.

The grasses were whipping back and forth, and the trees were being battered by wind. We watched as a branch from a mahogany tree came crashing down. But where we were standing, it was a quiet, windless day.

"What gives?" I asked out loud.

Connie shrugged.

"Well, maybe Mama Z can tell us," I said, and we walked a bit along the shoulder of the road until we got to the entrance of Little Boat Key, the next island over. There weren't any cars on the road, so it was a peaceful walk. Mama Z's sign welcomed us as we stepped onto a gravelly path that led to a wooden cottage painted in every imaginable color. The roof shingles were bright blue, the walls were purple, the porch was green, and the railing was pink. The window frames were red, and the front door was a bright, sunny yellow. A wind chime hung limply beside the door. It was made of ceramic eyes looking in every direction.

I stepped onto the porch, but Connie stayed put.

"What's wrong?"

"Ever heard of Hansel and Gretel? Two children, such as ourselves, find themselves in front of a candy-colored house, such as this. Then a witch eats them."

"That's just a fairy tale," I said. Mary Shelley lumbered up onto the porch with me.

"And I'm invisible. Stranger things have happened," Connie said, crossing her arms.

She had a point. But we'd already come all this way. "Mama Z is a business owner. It wouldn't pay for her to eat her customers," I argued.

Connie narrowed her eyes at me. "She can't eat me if she can't see me. But you, Frank, are completely visible. I'll leave a note for your parents if worse comes to worst."

A door knocker shaped like a mermaid was set into the center of the door. I lifted the bronze tail and rapped three times.

"Do you think she's home?" Connie whispered. She was holding tightly to Mary Shelley's collar now.

We waited a few minutes. I tried again, grabbing hold of the mermaid's tail. But suddenly, the door was yanked open and there stood a woman with hair dyed bright red and cut just above her shoulders. She had purple makeup on her eyelids and wore big earrings shaped like stingrays. Her dress was long and red, and she wore a bunch of colorful beaded necklaces.

"Buenas tardes," Mama Z boomed at us. Her voice was big, bigger even than my papi's and mom's when they were arguing. It made my ears ring a little.

"Hola," I said. "We're wondering if you can help us?"

"Us?" the woman asked.

Well, that was the first question answered. She didn't seem to notice Connie at all.

"Yes, Mama Z," I said. "That's the problem."

"I see," she said.

"You don't, actually," I added.

Mama Z fiddled with her beaded necklaces. "I am intrigued. Por favor, pasa," she said, and led us into her home. We walked through a lounge with two comfy sofas and a television and past a tiny kitchen with a huge bubbling pot on the stove.

"That's a big pot, Frank," Connie whispered behind me.

"Shush," I said.

Mama Z turned around. "¿Perdón?"

"Nothing!"

"This way, then," Mama Z said. Before us hung velvet curtains in emerald. Mama Z parted them to reveal a dining room. Inside was a round table with chairs all around. A crystal ball sat in the center, the diplomas that dotted the walls reflected in its glass. Mama Z seemed to have degrees in hypnosis, paranormal investigations, telepathy, and séances. She motioned to the chairs, and Connie and I sat down. Mary Shelley rested her head on my lap.

Mama Z cracked her knuckles, then twisted her head from side to side. Finally, she pointed to a sign on the wall between diplomas that read:

TAROT READINGS $50
SUMMONING THE DEAD $100
GENERAL ADVICE $30

I fished the money out of my pocket. "General advice, please."

"How much should we pay her not to boil us alive?" Connie muttered. I kicked her under the table.

Mama Z counted the bills and put the money in her dress pocket. "How can I help you?" she asked, resting her hands on the table with her palms up.

"I have a friend who can't remember who she is," I began.

Mama Z frowned. "Oh yes. It's hard as people age. They sometimes get forgetful."

"No, this friend is my age. I think." I faced Connie. "How old are you anyway?"

Connie brightened. "I know the answer to this one! I am eleven!"

I nodded and looked at Mama Z. "She's eleven, like me." I suppose I didn't stop to think what that conversation looked like to Mama Z. She probably thought I was playing a prank on her, which was definitely what I would have thought in her place.

Mama Z tapped her lips with a long red nail. At last she spoke. "I believe your friend has a bigger problem. She's invisible!"

"Yes. That, too!" I said, excited. Could it be that Mama Z actually believed me?

Connie scooted to the edge of her seat. "Tell her I'm not imaginary either!"

"She's not imaginary either!" I put in.

Mama Z grinned. "Muy bien, let's begin. Tell your friend to peer into the crystal ball. You too."

Connie and I leaned forward. Even Mary Shelley sat up and put her head on the table.

I saw nothing but Mama Z's big eyes, and her red lipstick, and her frizzy red hair, of course. Crystal balls weren't really magical. Everybody knew that.

"Now we will see if your friend is a ghost. Ghosts cannot resist crystal balls!"

Connie cried out, "I don't want to be a ghost, Frank! If I'm a ghost, that means I'm *dead*!"

Mama Z must have noticed that something was going on because she said, very quietly, "It's important to know the truth about things, even when the truth is hard."

"Okay," Connie said, wiping her eyes.

"Okay," I echoed.

I hadn't considered that Connie was a ghost. After all, she was solid. She'd grabbed my hand and squeezed it and I'd felt it. Ghosts were transparent, wispy things, made of . . . paranormal smoke or something. But that was just in books and movies. Ghosts weren't real. There was no science in the world that could prove they were.

I reached over and patted Connie's shoulder. "Don't worry," I whispered. "You aren't a ghost."

Connie nodded, dried her eyes with her apron, and sat up a little straighter than before.

We sat very patiently as Mama Z lit ten white candles, dimmed the lights, and called out.

"Little fantasma, heed my call. Do you feel compelled to speak today?" she asked in a booming voice.

"Is she talking to me?" Connie asked.

I knew that "fantasma" meant *ghost*. "I think so."

"Do you feel compelled to speak today?" Mama Z asked again in her loud voice.

"What does *compelled* mean?" I asked for both me and Connie.

"It means that you feel as if you MUST speak, or you might explode." Mama Z's breath fogged up the crystal ball.

Connie was quiet as she examined her feelings. "No, I do not feel compelled," she replied.

I said so to Mama Z, who wondered for a bit. "Ghosts must be called by their proper designations. ¿Como te llamas, fantasmita?" Mama Z asked at last.

"She doesn't know her real name," I said.

"Unlucky," Mama Z said. "Names are almighty things."

I thought about my own name. It didn't seem so almighty to me. If I could have, I would have named myself something else entirely. Like Hercules, maybe. Or Dracula. "She named herself Connie, after the element Zirconium." Connie was nodding vigorously beside me.

"Ah!" Mama Z exclaimed. "Naming *oneself* is even more powerful. Zirconium is a wonderfully scientific choice. Zircon crystals are clear and red, like rubies almost. Very beautiful."

I watched as Connie blushed pink all over her face.

"She says 'thank you,'" I told Mama Z, which earned me a scowl from Connie.

"Don't put words in my mouth, Frank," Connie scolded me. "But I am thankful."

"And her surname?" Mama Z asked.

I watched as Connie glanced around the room again, caught sight of a calendar, and made a choice.

"Friday," she said.

"Zirconium 'Connie' Friday." I repeated it to Mama Z.

"Un placer, Connie Friday," Mama Z said. "Now, back to the task at hand. I don't believe your friend is a ghost."

"See? I told you!" I said to Connie, who beamed at me.

Mama Z cleared her throat. "But I must think up one more experiment to be sure. First, though, snacks!"

Connie squeaked beside me. "Here it comes. The Hansel and Gretel part of the story!"

But Mama Z reached under the table and brought out a box of store-bought granola bars. "Sometimes clients feel a little woozy after a session. These get the blood sugar right up," she said.

I chose a chocolate chip bar for myself, but Connie shook her head. While I ate, Mama Z stood up and started to tinker with a machine that looked like a printer. It was sitting on a little table off to the side of the room. "This is a spectrometer, which is a machine that splits light into wavelengths," Mama Z explained.

I got excited at that. *A real spectrometer,* I thought. Pop-Pop had shown me one once in his lab. *Now we were getting somewhere.*

"It is well known that ghosts glow in the dark and, hence, produce a particular form of illumination," Mama Z continued. She pointed at her séance degree and said, "I have long studied the paranormal arts. Now, where is your friend?"

I pointed at Connie, who sat up as if she were having her picture taken.

"Little fantasma, come stand over here, por favor," Mama Z said.

Connie rose. She glanced at me over her shoulder, took a deep breath, and faced the machine.

"She's ready," I said.

Mama Z aimed her spectrometer at Connie. The machine whirred for a moment, while a tiny green light blinked on and off. Mama Z read the results off a little screen.

"Hmm," Mama Z said. "The spectrometer does not detect any ghostly light."

Connie turned and stuck her tongue out at me. "See! I knew I wasn't a ghost!"

"One more experiment, then! And for this, I need your pooch. What is your perrita's name?" Mama Z asked.

She needed my dog? For the first time since we'd been in Mama Z's cottage, I got nervous. Then I remembered that Mary Shelley was the size of a small horse. It's not like Mama Z could dognap her or anything.

"Mary Shelley," I said.

Mama Z lifted an eyebrow at that. "Ah! You named her after the creator of science fiction! This must be a very smart dog."

"She is," Connie and I said at the same time, which made me feel all warm inside for some reason.

"Okay. We begin. Fantasmita, please call for Mary Shelley," Mama Z boomed. She seemed to only use that voice when talking to Connie, as if she were trying to communicate from inside a bank vault.

Connie rolled her shoulders, gripped her apron, and then said, "Mary Shelley! Come here, you beautiful creature!"

Mary Shelley crawled under the table, emerged on the other side to reach Connie, then rolled onto her back for a belly rub. Connie got on her knees to give her a good scratch, saying, "You always do everything right, Mary Shelley. Yes, you do. You're a very good dog indeed."

Mama Z began to laugh. "There is your answer! Dogs never listen to ghost commands. Dogs are here amid the living to teach us lessons about goodness. Your friend is no ghost, but she *is* invisible, and I do not know why." Mama Z walked over to where Connie was, stopping just a few feet away. Then she got on her knees so that she and Connie were face-to-face. "Connie, it won't be easy going through life without anybody but him seeing you."

"Will I become visible again?" Connie asked. Tears fell down her cheeks, dripped onto her legs, and slid into her red-laced boots. I repeated the question for Mama Z.

Mama Z only shrugged. "I do not know, mi cielo."

"If I remain invisible," she asked, "how will I be of use in the world?"

Again I asked Connie's question, and Mama Z exclaimed, "Of use? What a thing to say! A person doesn't ever need to be 'of use.' A person ought only to love and be loved."

"But nobody loves me," Connie said. "Nobody even remembers me!" I didn't repeat that because there was a lump in my throat.

Mama Z looked at the place where Connie stood. She reached out and patted the air, missing the top of Connie's head by a few inches. But Connie closed her eyes anyway and seemed grateful for the gesture.

"How come only I can see her, then?" I asked. Part of me was afraid that I'd imagined the whole thing. It was the only logical answer. But then I felt Connie grip my hand and squeeze.

Mama Z thought for a moment. "The only thing I can say for sure is that you and Connie were meant to help one another, the way good friends always do," she told me. "Now it is time for you to go. I have soup on the stove and I don't want it to burn."

Chapter 11

THE ARRIVAL OF SOMETHING ELSE

"I'm not sure if that was useful or not," Connie said as we stepped off Mama Z's front porch. "But I'm glad Mama Z didn't eat us."

"Me too," I admitted. Connie was right. We still didn't have any real answers about why she was invisible. "I'm also still not sure this isn't heatstroke, to be honest," I said. It was even hotter now than it had been when we'd first arrived. The granola I'd eaten felt like it was doing flips in my stomach. I'd taken one for Connie when Mama Z wasn't looking and offered it to her now.

Connie ran her fingers over the glossy wrapper. She opened the bar carefully, then folded the wrapper and put it in her apron pocket. "It's so shiny and beautiful," she said. Connie ate the granola bar, munching away and making

"Mm-mm," sounds, but her snack never seemed to get any smaller. Eventually, it slipped from her hands, forgotten. I kicked it into the grass so that Mary Shelley wouldn't snarf it down and make herself sick.

A hot-pink convertible rumbled down the road, music blasting.

Connie stopped to stare. "I've never seen an automobile like that. Or like that, or that," she added, pointing to various cars in the distance. "At least, I don't remember having seen one."

Now it was my turn to stop and stare. Everything about Connie was strange—the way she talked, the clothes she wore, the things she found fascinating. The fact that she said *automobile* instead of *car*. Being invisible was the least weird thing about her, in my opinion. Mama Z said she wasn't a ghost, and I agreed with her. Connie said she didn't feel like a ghost, and she definitely didn't want to be one, so what was she?

Maybe if I asked her the right questions as we walked, it would jog her memory.

"Connie, what's your favorite color?" I figured I'd start with an easy question.

"Blue, like the sea," she said brightly.

"Favorite animal?"

Connie smirked, then gave Mary Shelley a pat. "This one! Mary Shelley is my favorite animal, bar none."

"Favorite movie?"

She gave a sad shrug. "Never been to a cinema, as far as I can recall."

"How is that even possible?" I said, throwing my hands in the air. "Even if you haven't gone to a movie theater, you can stream one online."

She clapped her hands and said, "Oh yes, I've seen streams, I think. I have a memory of walking into one. The water was cool between my toes, and there was a salamander there, too. A memory, Frank! Thank you!" Connie stopped and hugged me hard.

I was glad she'd remembered something, but she'd really missed the point, hadn't she?

An idea was starting to tickle my brain, one that made me afraid to ask my next question.

"I'm glad you're remembering," I said, peeling her arms off me. "One more question: Who's the president of the United States?"

Connie squeezed her eyes shut in concentration. "Um. Hang on. It starts with an *H*." Then she snapped her fingers. "Herbert Hoover, that's the one!"

Back in the fourth grade, I'd memorized the US presidents in a song I'd seen on a cartoon. It took me over a week, but once their names were burned into my brain, I couldn't get them out. Herbert Hoover wasn't even halfway through the song!

"That's nowhere near right," I whispered. Then I asked the big question. "What year were you born, Connie?"

She crossed her arms and gave me a look like I was

bananas. "We're both eleven. You should know this, Frank. We were born in 1921." She tsked at me and kept walking with Mary Shelley, leaving me standing there with my mouth hanging open.

1921.

1921?

Connie Friday was either over one hundred years old, or she was a time traveler. . . .

Or maybe, just maybe, Mama Z had been wrong and Connie really was a ghost.

If so, it was going to break her heart.

As for me, my brain felt like it was going to break in half. I believed in science, and in science, there was no room for ghosts from the beyond. But Connie was invisible, and she was born too long ago to be believed—plus, there was that weird thing that happened whenever she "ate." The evidence was stacking up in the ghost column. Even a scientist couldn't ignore that.

When I'd done that experiment back at the abandoned building, had I accidentally zapped Connie back from the beyond? And if I did, if it was my fault that she was trapped here, would she ever forgive me?

I ran to catch up to Connie, but as I did, we heard a gasping noise behind us.

Connie, Mary Shelley, and I turned around to see Mama Z running toward us, clasping her side with one hand and gulping for air.

"You're so fast," she panted as she reached us. Then she held out her other hand, which clutched Bernard, the haunted doll. "You forgot your muñeco."

Mary Shelley barked happily, yanking Bernard from Mama Z's hand.

"Th-thanks," I stuttered, my heart pounding. How had Bernard gotten to Mama Z's cottage?

"De nada," Mama Z said, catching her breath. She smoothed her hair and straightened the beads around her neck. "Ah sí, and then there was this, too." Mama Z pulled a note out from her pocket and handed it to me.

Taking a deep breath, I unfolded the piece of paper.

I SAID HELP.
CAN'T YOU READ, FARNK?

"Not again," Connie whispered at my side.

Mama Z peered at the note in my hands, and then a very serious look came over her face. "You aren't alone," she announced.

"I know," I told her, pointing at Connie.

"Not her. There's something else." Mama Z looked all around, as if this "something else" might appear. Suddenly, a fruity smell filled the air, as if someone was eating a Popsicle nearby.

"What? What else is there?" I demanded.

Mama Z wrinkled her nose. "I don't think the tooth fairy

has given you enough money for that answer."

"But that's not helpful at all!" I cried.

Mama Z ignored me and left the way she came, calling out, "Adios, niño. Adios, niña. Adios, perrita, and adios to the other one."

Connie and I watched her go in silence until she was just a speck in the distance. Mary Shelley had settled into the grass with Bernard, snuffling him all over.

"I'm scared, Frank," Connie said.

"Me too," I admitted. "Do you smell that?"

Connie nodded. "Mm-hmm. Sweet. Like candy."

Then we both heard it, as if there were a person standing between us—

A loud and wet *sniff*.

"I'd like to run very fast now," Connie said quietly.

I nodded, and we took off with Mary Shelley bounding behind us, all the way back to the lighthouse.

Chapter 12

THE SPOTTED WHALE ALL-YOU-CAN-EAT BUFFET

By the time we reached the lighthouse we were gulping for air like fish out of water. The afternoon sun was blazingly hot, and I was sweating all over. Climbing the steps to my room had made my muscles burn. Even Mary Shelley was worn out. The sweet smell had followed us all the way to Spectacle Key, but was carried away by the wind as soon as the abandoned house came into view.

Mary Shelley had carried Bernard with her and settled the doll on her dog bed, giving it a doggy look that said *stay.*

"What do you think Mama Z meant about 'something else'?" I wondered out loud.

"I really don't know. But it felt like we weren't alone, didn't it?"

Nodding, I scanned the room. It was the same as I'd left

it. I'd say it was normal, but there was nothing normal about the lighthouse or the island. Just then, a remote-control car zipped out of my closet, did a U-turn, and put itself away.

Connie and I both yelped.

"Who set off your windup car?" Connie whispered.

I picked up the car, turned it around, and popped off the cover to the batteries. *No batteries.* My hands shook as I showed it to Connie. "Nobody," I said, and chucked the car back into the closet.

"And we know what Bernard can do," Connie said, eyeing the doll suspiciously.

Downstairs, I heard Papi let loose a string of curses aimed at the water heater. Mom answered with a few colorful words of her own.

"Then there's that," I said with a sigh.

Connie looked thoughtful. "Mama Z said we were meant to help one another. Perhaps that's why I left the dark place where I was and came here. To help you figure out the problem with Spectacle Key."

"And maybe I can help you not be invisible anymore," I said.

"Partners, then," Connie said, extending her hand. I shook it, and it felt like we'd taken a step toward a plan, even though we didn't really have one yet.

My eyes fell on the bookcase, full of books in which all kinds of inexplicable things happened—monsters, ghosts, curses. Beside the bookcase, in the duffel bag on the floor, was Pop-Pop's chemistry set. The scientist and the story lover in me felt like they were at war in my brain. It was like I'd stepped into a horror story, one where science didn't have the answers. But that couldn't be right. It just wasn't possible!

Spectacle Key had me really messed up.

I started thinking how weird it was that my first real friend was possibly a ghost. Living or . . . not living, I liked spending time with Connie, even if everything about her situation was strange and getting spookier by the minute.

Connie flopped onto my bed and stretched out like a starfish. When her fingers brushed the pages of the proof I'd been working on, she sat up and asked, "What's this?"

"A proof. It's like an argument on the page that a scientist has with himself. I mean, other people can read it, too. But it's a way of arranging your thoughts about something that's hard to understand."

"Oh. Like my invisibility. And Spectacle Key's mysteries."

"Let's list everything we know," I said, tearing a fresh page out of the notebook I kept on my nightstand. I wrote:

Problems with Spectacle Key

My friend Connie is invisible and we don't know why.

Connie read over my shoulder. "I'm a *problem?*"

"No," I said quickly. "But your invisibility is, right?"

"Yes, it very much is a problem. My bad memory is a problem, too, Frank."

I add Connie's amnesia to the list.

Connie can't remember anything except walking in a stream once.

"That's good," Connie said. "You should write something about your parents being so cross with one another all the time."

I jotted down:

Mom and Papi can't stop fighting about everything.

"How about the weather? It's bonkers here," I said.

Connie nodded, then snapped her fingers. "Don't forget about Snuffles!"

"Snuffles?" I asked.

"Mm-hmm. 'The other one' that Mama Z mentioned. Whoever they are, they sniffled all the way to Spectacle Key. Must have caught a cold."

I could already tell that Connie was the kind of person who worried about others. A possibly evil spirit had chased us. Who else would care if it was feeling under the weather? It made me like her even more. I penciled in:

Snuffles. Evil? Or a disembodied cold?

"There's also the sweet smell. I've noticed that for a while now," I said. "And the messages with my name misspelled."

"And don't forget Bernard," Connie said, shivering all over.

I wrote:

A sweet smell is in the air. Why?

Who is leaving the "Farnk" notes?

Bernard, the (probably) Haunted Doll

Connie and I reread the list. "That's everything," Connie said, and started unlacing her boots. She pulled them off, and they fell to the floor with clear thuds. I wondered if my parents, bickering faintly downstairs, could hear them, too.

"Yep, I guess we listed everything," I lied. Connie's boots had reminded me: she'd said her birthday was in 1921, over a hundred years ago. If Connie wasn't a time traveler, and she wasn't a ghost, then what was she?

If Connie had traveled through time, and had somehow forgotten how or why she'd done it, that meant there was a family back in the past waiting for her. Missing her.

But if Connie was a ghost, it meant she'd died, probably long ago considering her clothes and everything she didn't recognize around her. She'd almost panicked when Mama Z mentioned the possibility that she might be a spirit. Maybe Mama Z had lied. Maybe Connie really was a ghost, and Mama Z had only spared her feelings.

And if Connie was a ghost, then what or who was Snuffles? Were they a ghost, too?

I could have thought about these questions all day, going round and round in my head and getting nowhere, but Mom's voice shook me out of it.

"Frankie! Come down quick, mister! There's a surprise for you!" she shouted.

Ugh, no more surprises, I thought. But when I got to the bottom of the stairs, with Connie and Mary Shelley right behind me, I changed my mind.

"Pop-Pop!" I shouted, and jumped off the final step with a big leap.

"Sonny boy!" Pop-Pop said in return. He always called me "sonny boy," and sometimes, he called my mom his "sonny girl," which always made her laugh. "I'm hankering for some seafood," Pop-Pop said, rubbing his big belly. He was wearing a University of Miami T-shirt like he always did, khaki shorts, socks pulled halfway up his calves, and white sneakers. Pop-Pop's wispy blond hair barely covered his head. I was thrilled to see him. He was the only grandparent I had. Mom's mother, my grandma Eleanor, had died before I was born, and Papi's parents had passed away in Cuba a long time ago, too. I was always a little jealous of kids who had all four of their grandparents around. They didn't know how lucky they were.

I felt a tug on my sleeve and Connie started whispering, "I'm having a memory, Frank! Of my own grandaddy! He was very short but very strong, and he smoked a pipe! Your pop-pop takes after him."

"That's great, Connie!" I said, glad that another memory had come to her.

"What's great?" Pop-Pop asked.

Mom interrupted. "Daddy, Frankie is talking to his imaginary friend."

I could feel my cheeks burning. Behind me, Connie grumbled.

Pop-Pop's eyebrows rose. "Is that so? Well, your momma

had an imaginary friend, too, and so did I."

"What?" I asked, surprised. Pop-Pop was a scientist! He'd never believe in imaginary people!

"Can we talk about it over lunch?" Papi asked, motioning to the front door. His stomach grumbled loudly in support.

We piled into the van—Mom, Papi, Pop-Pop, Connie, and me. Pop-Pop had his cell phone out and was shouting directions at Papi.

"It's one road, Jim. North and south. We can't get lost," Papi was saying, but Pop-Pop ignored him.

Meanwhile, Connie had scrambled up to the front of the car, having slipped right out of her seat belt. She was leaning on the dashboard between Papi and Pop-Pop, her palms flat on the front windshield. I wanted to tell her that was *way* not safe, but I didn't want the "imaginary friend" conversation to start up again.

"There it is, boy-o!" Pop-Pop shouted, pointing at a restaurant with a glittery sign that read *The Spotted Whale All-You-Can-Eat Buffet*. "Take a louie!" which was what Pop-Pop always said when he meant, "Go left." A giant gray whale covered in sequin polka dots seemed to swim over the restaurant roof. Its back was faded from the sunlight, but it was still pretty impressive.

I waited for Connie while my family walked ahead of me.

"Your automobile goes so fast!" she said, her eyes big and shiny.

"They do in my time," I said under my breath.

"What was that?" Connie asked.

"Nothing. Let's eat. I'm starving." Connie shrugged, letting my comment go.

At some point, I would have to tell her that I thought she actually was a ghost, but I didn't know how to break it to her. It was the only explanation for what was going on. Connie was invisible, she ate but her food didn't really get eaten, she said she was born over a hundred years ago, and her memory of her life was almost entirely gone. Mama Z *must* have been lying to us. Connie Friday was a ghost. I'd bet anything.

I'd just have to find a way to tell her . . . gently.

Then we'd figure out why she'd come back. Ghosts always returned with a mission, didn't they? At least, that was always the case with the spirits in my books and comics. It usually had to do with their death. Sometimes, they came back for revenge. But Connie didn't seem the vengeful type.

I watched as Connie skipped into the restaurant, slipping in right behind Pop-Pop. I followed her. She paused to look at everything—the red vinyl booths, the long buffet tables, the waitstaff in their crisp black aprons, and the bubbling, brightly lit jukebox in one corner. Her eyes were wide and her mouth was open. What had Connie come back for, anyway? A tour of the twenty-first century? There *had* to be something else, something I was missing.

"Boo!" I heard behind me at the same time that a pair of hands grabbed my shoulders.

I shouted and turned around, my heart beating a million

miles an hour, only to be faced with a red-haired kid my age, wearing a mask in the shape of a stingray.

"It's me, Lucas, remember?" Lucas said, pulling the stingray mask off. "The servers give masks to all the kids. I wanted a shark but all they've got left are these ones. Hey, wanna play in the arcade?"

"No thanks," I told Lucas, and rushed off to join my family at a big table with bench seats. I didn't trust that kid. And even though it looked more and more like I was dealing with something supernatural on Spectacle Key, I still wasn't completely convinced that Lucas wasn't trying to prank me.

Back at our table, Pop-Pop had already put on a plastic bib with a cartoon lobster on it and a server was going around filling cups of water. "For you, sweetheart," the server said, and dropped a stingray mask on the table. I looked across the restaurant, where Lucas was giving me a thumbs-up. I pushed the mask to the center of the table.

"So where's your imaginary pal sitting?" Pop-Pop asked.

I groaned. Not this again. "Over there," I said. Connie waved at Pop-Pop, but he didn't see her, of course.

"What's his name, then?" Pop-Pop asked. Papi was watching with narrowed eyes. I knew he didn't like this one bit. Meanwhile, Mom was smiling an *Isn't my son adorable?* smile at me.

"Connie. *Her* name is Connie," I said.

Pop-Pop tried to hide a smile. "Is she old or young?"

"She's a kid like me, Pop-Pop," I said, sinking down lower

in my seat. Did the earth ever really swallow people up? Because right now I hoped it would gulp me down.

Pop-Pop tipped an imaginary hat at her and said, "Nice to make your acquaintance, young lady." Then he pointed a fork at my mom. "This one here had a young gentleman as her imaginary friend, if I recall. I had one, too. He broke my toys and pencils and such. Naughty boy," Pop-Pop said very seriously. "What is your friend like?"

"I'm delightful. But confused, sir," Connie answered Pop-Pop.

"She's delightfully confused. All the time," I said.

That's when Papi slammed his hands on the table and shouted, "DOES NOBODY THINK THIS IS WEIRD? AT ALL? IS IT A KEYS THING BECAUSE YA NO PUEDO CON ESTAS LOCURAS!"

It felt like half the restaurant stopped to stare at us. Even Lucas and his mother, Emily Shiverton, and everyone at their table craned their necks to look. But they only looked for a moment before Ms. Shiverton rose and headed our way. Three other people joined her—two white women wearing matching pink blouses, and a Black man in a bow tie.

"Look what you did," my mom whispered angrily. "You've sicced HAUNT on us just when we were going to have a nice dinner with Daddy." Mom turned around and with a huge smile on her face said, "Emilyyyyy, so nice to see you. Have you tried the scallops?"

"Joooooyce," Ms. Shiverton said. "Allow me to introduce three of HAUNT's founding members—Minnie and

Winnie Watson, twins as you can see, and Mark McPhee. We were just going over your case."

"Our case?" Papi asked.

Mr. McPhee cleared his throat. "Yes. The legality of the occupation permit for the Spectacle Key lighthouse is in question."

Papi got to his feet. "There's no question. We occupy it. Punto y aparte."

"'Punto y aparte' means *And that's that!*" I translated for Pop-Pop.

"The question is not whether you live there. It's whether you should," one of the twins trilled.

"A historical building such as your own requires thoughtful caretakers," chimed in the other twin.

"Listen, Emily. We all know you put in an offer to buy the lighthouse at the same time we did. But we had the higher bid. That's how the real estate cookie crumbles sometimes," Mom said in the kind of voice that meant business.

"Your case is before the mayor," Ms. Shiverton added, completely unbothered by what my mom had said.

Now it was Mom's turn to stand up. "What mayor? Spectacle Key doesn't have a mayor!"

The members of HAUNT all started to laugh. "Of course it does," Ms. Shiverton said. Then she and the others returned to their table.

Mom and Papi sat down in slow motion and started murmuring about lawyers.

Pop-Pop nudged me in the ribs. "Let's go fill up our plates

before they change their minds about eating here. These licorice sticks won't carry me through the day," he said, pointing to the candy bulge in his shirt pocket. Mom always kept caramels in her purse. That day, I had a lollipop in my left pocket. The sweet tooth ran in the family.

"An excellent idea!" Connie said, running to the buffet. She loaded her plate with crab claws, salad, hunks of mahi-mahi, steaming mussels, and even a few California rolls. "I don't know what this is, but it smells so good!" she chattered. Nobody else noticed her as she walked back to the table with a heaping plate of food.

I worried that somebody might see a plate floating in midair, but somehow, Connie managed to zigzag between hungry customers and waiters rushing about without being noticed. I wondered if the things she touched went invisible, too. We'd have to run an experiment later. At one point, a busboy backed into her, sending her plate crashing down.

Connie stomped her foot in frustration and went back to the buffet for more, while the busboy cursed under his breath and picked up the mess.

Pop-Pop and I made our selections, too. Mine was all coconut shrimp and Pop-Pop's was all crab legs.

"Pop-Pop," I asked as we looked at the dessert options at the end of the buffet table, "back when you were a scientist, did—"

"I'm still one, sonny boy. Always will be," he said, tapping his temple with his free hand.

"Right," I said. "Which is why I'm wondering: What do you do if you can't believe your own eyes and ears?"

Pop-Pop stopped and thought for a moment. He squinted into the distance, as if the answer was far away, over by the emergency exits or something. I loved watching Pop-Pop think. It was like his brain went into download mode as he searched for an answer.

"First off," he said at last, "make sure you've eliminated all the possibilities for the unbelievable thing."

"Got it. Did that. Mostly," I said.

"Then go to the source. Where were you when the unbelievable thing first happened? Try to re-create the moment!" Pop-Pop said, swinging a crab leg for emphasis. A waiter looked at him with a scowl. "All experiments need to be run several times in order to verify the results."

Go to the source? That meant returning to the abandoned house where I'd first met Connie!

"Interesting," I said. "What else?"

Pop-Pop laughed. "Sonny boy, at that point if you find that you're still dealing with something unbelievable, well then, you'd better start believing it."

Chapter 13

VIDEO GAMES AND NOT-SO-FUNNY PRANKS

When we returned to the table, Mom and Papi were very quiet.

"Aren't y'all going to eat?" Pop-Pop asked, setting his plate down.

Connie's face was shiny with butter and she was leaning back and rubbing her stomach with her eyes closed. Her food, however, appeared untouched.

Mom noticed it and started picking at some shrimp. "Who brought the extra plate?" she asked. "Here, eat up," she said, and pushed the plate toward Papi.

"I don't have much of an appetite now."

"No appetite?" Pop-Pop asked, then shoved fried squid from Connie's plate into his mouth.

"Who can blame me? We might have to leave Spectacle Key," Papi moaned. Mom nodded sadly. Even though she seemed to hate Spectacle Key, she didn't want Papi's dream to crash and burn.

At that, Connie opened her eyes and sat upright. "Tell them you can't, Frank! You can't leave me on the island by myself!" She sprang to her feet and ran off.

"Excuse me," I said. Mom and Papi were so down in the dumps they didn't even notice me going. I chased Connie all the way to the arcade, where she stopped in front of a video game called Hurricane Hero. Lucas was playing. He was sitting on a bench with a seat belt strapped around his chest and lap. His hands were on a wheel, and the screen showed him driving a big bus with monster-truck wheels on it! The bus flew down a rainy road, while wind seemed to batter the town around it. Every so often, a character would stand at the side of the road calling for help, and Lucas would have to pump the brake to let them on. Then off he went again, speeding down highways, dodging falling trees and sudden tornadoes. The bench Lucas sat on rumbled and bounced, which was why he needed the seat belt.

Even though I didn't like video games, this one was pretty cool.

But Connie? She hated it. She, too, was watching Lucas play, but her hands were covering her mouth, and her eyes were wide and full of tears. Every so often, a full-body shiver seemed to take her over.

"I've never been so scared," Connie said to me when I got close to her.

"It's just a game. A dumb video game," I told her.

Connie shook her head. "No, it's real, Frank. It's terrifying."

Lucas rode his bus over a crumbling bridge. The game's audio was full of the sounds of screaming people. Connie clamped her hands over her ears.

"Connie, are you having a memory?" I asked. She didn't answer. Instead, she closed her eyes tightly and kept on covering her ears.

The game ended when the timer ran out. "Guess the storm's got me," Lucas said. Connie was weeping loudly. The game didn't seem so cool anymore. When he saw me standing there, Lucas dug a video game token out of his pocket. "Here, wanna play with me?" he asked.

"No thanks. I gotta go," I said.

Lucas shrugged. "Maybe next time."

"Yeah," I said, though what I meant was *no* and *never*. Lucas's mother was actively trying to get my family kicked out of our home!

Connie and I headed out of the arcade. Her head hung low, and she bumped into me from time to time. "Promise you won't leave me, Frank. Everybody leaves me."

"That can't be true," I said, but Connie nodded quickly. "Another memory?" Connie shook her head.

"Just a feeling," she said.

"I won't leave," I promised, though I wasn't sure it was a promise I could actually keep. I was always the kid leaving at the end of the school year and never coming back. Then I heard Lucas call my name.

"Hey, Frank! You forgot your doll," he said. Lucas held Bernard at the waist.

I felt myself shaking all over. So, it *was* Lucas playing a prank on me!

"YOU!" I shouted, and marched over to Lucas. "YOU THINK YOU'RE FUNNY?"

Lucas lifted his hands and started backing away. "It's okay, bro. I have a stuffed rabbit I sleep with. Your doll's kinda cute," he said, thrusting Bernard at me.

"YOU CAN'T SCARE ME OR MY FAMILY OFF THE ISLAND," I continued to shout.

Lucas threw Bernard and I caught it. "I don't know what you're talking about," he said. "I found it over by Hurricane Hero!"

Connie was talking, but I couldn't hear her over the roaring in my ears. "Frank. Frank, stop. Listen, can't you hear it?" she was saying.

I stopped. Listened. The restaurant was playing 80s music, and people chattered while they ate. Forks and knives clinked against plates, and Lucas was breathing hard.

But underneath all that was the continuous sound of somebody sniffling.

"Snuffles is back," Connie whispered. She gripped my wrist in fear. I knew why. Snuffles *was* creepy, showing up out of the blue, following us around even if we couldn't see him.

That's when I smelled it, too. Something sweet was overpowering the seafood smells in the air.

The commotion I'd made with my shouting had called

attention to us. Soon my mom was standing behind me, and Ms. Shiverton had her hands on Lucas's shoulders.

"Everything okay here, mister?" Mom asked.

"Yeah, fine," I said a little too loudly.

"Yep," Lucas said, though his ears were red and his hands were curled into fists.

Ms. Shiverton made a squeaky and judgmental sound in the back of her throat. Then she led her son away.

"Seriously," Mom said when they were out of earshot. "Everything okay?"

I watched Lucas go. Now that I'd busted him with Bernard, he'd stop messing with me. At least, I hoped so.

"What if it isn't him?" Connie was asking beside me. "What if the doll is haunted?"

Snuffles sniffed loudly at that.

"It's fine, Mom," I said at last. "Can we go home? I don't think I want to come back to this place ever again."

Mom laughed. "Tell that to Pop-Pop," she said, pointing at my grandfather, who had a pile of empty snow crab shells taller than he was on the table.

"They really were tasty," Connie said, smacking her lips.

Beside us, Snuffles breathed noisily again.

What had Pop-Pop said? That if I couldn't trust my eyes and ears, I'd better start believing. It was interesting that Pop-Pop, the best scientist I knew, felt that science didn't have all the answers all the time. But was I ready to start believing in ghosts and haunted dolls? There had to be a reason for everything happening on Spectacle Key, didn't there?

Chapter 14

CONNIE'S LULLABY

It was dark when we got back to Spectacle Key, and Pop-Pop had to go back to Miami.

"I'll visit again soon," he told me, giving me a crushing hug.

"Do you have to go?" I asked.

Pop-Pop took a long look at me. "You okay, Frank?"

For a second, I thought I might start crying. My eyes stung and my throat felt tight. But I swallowed it all back. Nothing I could say would make sense to Pop-Pop or to anybody.

"M'okay," I mumbled.

Pop-Pop raised an eyebrow. "Tell you what. I'll be back next week and the two of us can hang out, maybe run an experiment or two with that chemistry set I sent you."

"Promise?" I asked. Just the thought of spending time with Pop-Pop made me feel lighter.

"I never break a promise!" Pop-Pop said, and gave me another hug.

We all watched him go from the front door, waving goodbye as he drove off, his car getting tinier and tinier. I watched until I couldn't see him anymore. My parents went into the lighthouse, but Connie and I stayed outside.

"I like your grandfather very much," Connie said. "He's clever and kind."

I nodded. Pop-Pop was more than that. He was also brilliant and really generous. He always gave me half his desserts, and the coins in his pocket, and he used to take me to the zoo all the time, where he'd point out the differences between the plains zebra and the mountain zebra, or the patterns the meerkats made coming in and out of their dens. Pop-Pop told corny jokes and never asked me whether I'd made any friends at school. He was the closest thing I had to a friend.

That is, before Connie appeared out of nowhere.

In the distance, waves made slapping sounds and the breeze rustled the palm fronds. It was dark out, so the sea looked like a black blanket stretched out to infinity. I realized I was still holding Bernard under my shirt. I pulled him out and heard the tiniest little sniff in my ear. The wind picked up. Each time a gust flattened the grasses, Connie startled.

"Can we go inside?" she asked fearfully.

"Okay." Mom and Papi had turned off most of the lights downstairs, so we bumped into boxes and furniture as we went. Papi had plugged in some seashell nightlights, which cast strange, flickering shadows on the walls. It made the lighthouse feel alive in a different way—like it was watching us move through it.

I hurried up the stairs, two at a time.

Back in my room, Mary Shelley was sound asleep on my bed, snoring and drooling all over my pillow.

"Ew," I said, which woke her up. She launched herself off the bed and tackled me, licking me until my hair was standing up. "Here, here, take this," I shouted, shoving Bernard in Mary Shelley's face. Happy, she took the doll at last and settled down with it in her own bed.

Connie was in hysterics. "Look at your hair! It's disgusting!"

"You can stop laughing now," I said, grabbing a towel and wiping my face.

"You look like you've jumped into a vat of syrup," Connie said, snorting.

"Well, you look like a . . . like a—" I got stuck. Connie just looked like a kid. A kid from a long time ago, but just a kid.

Connie sat down on the window seat and faced me. She swung her boots back and forth, knocking the heels against the wall. "I know I don't look like you or that other boy, Lucas," Connie said. "I probably don't look like any of your friends."

"I don't have any friends, so it doesn't matter what you look like," I said softly.

Connie bolted upright. "That's impossible. You're you!

Funny and smart. Why wouldn't a boy like you have friends?"

I'm pretty sure I blushed right down to my toes, and very nearly blurted, *You're funny and smart, too!* but kept it under control. "My family moves so often that I never get to make any," I confessed. It hurt to say it out loud to anyone other than my parents. I never had before.

Connie looked at me with wide eyes. "You aren't moving away again, are you?" She'd started fiddling with one of her braids nervously.

"My parents promised we could stay here, but I don't know. Promises, right? They get broken." I hated how my voice cracked a little when I spoke just then, so I flipped open a nearby book and riffled through it thoughtlessly.

"Promises," Connie repeated. After a while, she asked, "I'm not . . . right, am I, Frank?"

I didn't know what to say to that. Maybe Connie was starting to suspect that she was a spirit, even if it was the last thing she wanted to be true.

"Connie, that video game that scared you back at the restaurant. Did you remember something?" I asked softly.

Connie took a deep breath. "Just wind, Frank. And rain. My face all wet and darkness so deep you could reach out and weigh it in in your hands. Maybe it was a memory. A scary one. I'm sorry I fell apart like that."

I felt tense all over, and even though I didn't know exactly what to say, I remembered something my mom always told me. "You don't have to apologize for feeling stuff. They're your feelings, after all."

She leaned her head against the window. "Frank, just now, I think I had another memory." Connie closed her eyes. "I can see a small house, somewhere thick with pines. There's a dark-haired woman at the stove, stirring a pot of something so wonderful I can taste it. When she looks at me with her deep brown eyes, I know she loves me. Could that be my momma?"

I didn't know what to say. I tried to imagine describing Mom that way. What would I say? That she was tall, wore shorts, and had freckles all over, even on her knees. When Mom looked at me, even when she was mad, I knew she loved me, too. As for Papi, he had dark hair like me, and brown eyes that were nearly black. He wore thick glasses and he and Mom were the same height. Sometimes when Papi looked at me, I could tell that he was thinking about tomorrow, and the day after that, and the day after that, full of hope for me and our family.

"That's a nice memory," I told Connie.

"Do you think it could be a memory of my momma?"

"Might be, Connie. What else do you remember?"

Connie scrunched up her nose and kept her eyes tightly shut. "I don't know. She's all I see. She *must* be my momma. I don't know how I know it, but I do." Connie pulled her knees up and hugged herself. "Thinking about her makes my heart ache. Do you think she's . . . dead?"

I could tell that Connie and I were thinking the same thing. *How do you break bad news to a ghost?* I wondered. I'd start scientifically—with the facts. "Connie, what year did you say you were born again?"

"1921."

"That was over a hundred years ago, is the thing. Do you know what a cell phone is? Or the space shuttle?" I asked.

"Sounds like nonsense," Connie said softly.

I wished I could get up and give her a hug, but I didn't want to be weird or anything. Instead I said, "I think Mama Z was wrong."

Connie looked at me with wide, damp eyes. "Y-you think I'm a ghost, don't you?"

"I've run out of scientific explanations. And Pop-Pop says once that happens, you have to start believing in the weird stuff. I do think you're a ghost. And I think there must be a reason you've returned. Think, Connie! What happened to you? Why have you come back?" I held back another question because I wasn't sure I actually wanted an answer—*Connie, how did you die?*

The wind started to howl even more loudly outside. Mary Shelley got up and nuzzled Connie, who had started to shiver. It seemed to give her strength. How come my dog was better at comforting people than I was?

"I don't remember enough to answer your questions, but as scary as it is, I'm starting to agree with you. Also, I think your grandfather was onto something, Frank. He said to start at the place where the unbelievable thing happened. We need to go back to that old building." Connie trembled all over.

Downstairs, we could hear my parents start yelling about a light bulb.

Connie and Pop-Pop were right. We had to return to the abandoned building. There were answers there, even if it was scary, even if someone or *something* was leaving me strange messages with my name misspelled over there.

"I've remembered something else," Connie said. She was facing the window now and staring at the ruin far in the distance. "It's a lullaby my momma sang to me."

Then Connie started to sing about a lonely breeze that zipped among pine trees on a beach, tickling the waves as it went. The melody wrapped itself around my brain until I felt I could hum along.

Connie sang softly, "*Ooh, ooh, ooh, ooh,*" tracing a finger over the moisture on the windowpane. Somehow, it was the saddest song I'd ever heard.

"I don't know what to say," I whispered, but I don't think Connie heard me. It felt like I'd known Connie for a long time. Was this what it was like for people who made friends easily?

Mary Shelley rested her head on Connie's lap as she sang, and her big eyes drooped. Connie would have drool all over her skirt soon, but I'm not sure that ghost clothes could get ruined. Connie's voice was a whisper now, but I could hear sadness in it, too.

Before I knew it, I started to drift off until I couldn't hear Connie or her momma's lullaby anymore.

Chapter 15

CONNIE IS GOOD AT NAMES

When I woke up the next morning, Connie was curled up on the rug beside my bed. She didn't even have a pillow. Mary Shelley was snuggled beside her, with Bernard sitting between her paws.

Some friend I was.

Without making a sound, I got up to take a shower and put on fresh clothes. When I returned to my room, Connie was looking through my closet.

"What's up?" I asked.

Slowly, Connie raised her eyes to the ceiling.

I couldn't help but laugh. "It means what are you up to?"

"Oh," she said. "Might I borrow your clothes? I think I'm quite ready to stop looking like a one-hundred-year-old."

I didn't tell her that I sort of liked her dress and her boots.

They made her unique. Instead I said, "Sure," and helped her pick through my T-shirts. Connie settled on a green shirt with a white alligator on the front. The words *See you later, alligator* were printed on the back. I'd gotten it last year on a trip to the Everglades with Pop-Pop. Connie slipped the shirt on over her dress.

"What do you think?" she asked.

"Cool," I said.

Connie looked puzzled. "Actually, I'm feeling a bit warm today." She cinched the T-shirt around her waist with a shoelace I'd left on the floor. "Perfect," she said, smoothing out the material.

Perfect, I thought, and gave her my biggest smile.

The T-shirt made me remember an experiment I'd thought up the day before. "Come with me," I said. Connie followed me up the stairs to where Papi was working on the lantern.

"Buenos días," Papi grumbled. There was a flashlight between his teeth while he tried to wrench a screw into place.

"Hey, Papi, check out my friend's new outfit," I said. Connie looked confused, but she grabbed the ends of the T-shirt and curtsied.

Papi looked our way and sighed. "M'ijo, you're too old for imaginary friends. I know Mom thinks that—"

"Bye, Papi!" I interrupted; then I grabbed Connie's hand and led her back to my bedroom.

She scowled at me. "What was that for?"

I sat on my bed and smiled, feeling very proud of myself. "An experiment to see if your invisibility extends to the things you touch. My Everglades shirt, your plate at the buffet, anything you actually hold, can't be seen by anyone but me." I thought for a minute. "But you did hold my hand and Papi didn't say that—"

"Frank Fernández!" Connie shouted. "Wipe that smug look off your face this instant. I am a person. A PERSON. Not an experiment for you to play scientist with."

"Play scientist?!" I repeated, my cheeks burning.

"Indeed," Connie said. She stomped both her boots, gave Bernard a vicious swipe that knocked him off the windowsill, then sat down.

Here's the thing about not having had many friends: I didn't know what to do when one of them was angry with me. I wasn't *playing scientist*. I was trying to learn as much as I could about Connie's situation. First my parents were bickering, and now me and Connie were fighting, too? So I did what my parents used to do when we didn't live on Spectacle Key. Before we came here, whenever they argued they always apologized to one another, and meant it.

"I'm sorry, Connie. I won't ever run an experiment on you again without asking first. And if you say no, I won't get mad. Pinkie promise?"

Connie's scowl slowly faded. "All right," she said, stuck out her pinkie finger, then recited:

"Pinkie, pinkie,
Whoever tells a lie
Will sink down to the bad place
And there they will die"

"Whoa, that's dark," I said, but linked my pinkie to hers anyway.

"It's daylight," Connie said, bewildered.

"I meant that rhyme. It's kind of depressing," I explained.

Connie laughed. "Do kids no longer make the pinkie promise swear?"

It was my turn to laugh. "Not like that. But I'm definitely using it from now on!" I was excited about the day, too. Pop-Pop had said we had to go back to the source. Maybe today we'd finally learn what was really going on with Connie.

"Here's the plan," I began. "First, breakfast. Preferably the most sugary cereal in the lighthouse. Then we go to the old building. Maybe something else will happen. Maybe you'll remember why you came back."

Connie grew very serious. "Frank, what if I go back there and can't leave? What if I disappear again? I'd stay here with you forever if I could."

That didn't sound so bad. Connie was great to have around. So what if everyone thought she was imaginary? Mary Shelley could see her, and that was good enough for me.

"I don't mind if you stay with me," I said quietly. Connie

blushed and I started fiddling with Mary Shelley's collar.

A loud and prolonged *sniiiiiffffff* interrupted my thinking.

"What about Snuffles?" Connie asked.

"What about them?" Whatever Snuffles was, they didn't seem to want anything except maybe allergy medicine. Still, whenever they made a sound, the little hairs on my arms stood on end.

"Is Snuffles a person? An island spirit? A breeze with a personality?" wondered Connie.

I thought for a moment. "Can't be a coincidence, can it? You coming back from wherever you were and Snuffles showing up at the same time."

"The windup car thing yesterday was extremely strange. Did Snuffles do that? And there are the Farnk messages, too," Connie wondered. "Who's writing *those*?"

Sniff, sniff, sniff, sniff.

Connie and I jumped at the noise. "If Snuffles is trying to tell us something, then there's an easy experiment for that," I said nervously, tearing a page out of a spiral notebook and setting a pen on top of it. "Snuffles? Are you leaving us messages?" I asked out loud.

"And misspelling Frank's name even after he told you the correct spelling. Honestly, Snuffles," Connie added.

Connie and I watched the pen and the paper for what felt like a long time. I steadied myself in case the pen started to twitch or something. Couldn't go screaming my head off at my own experiment. But nothing happened. Snuffles didn't make a sound. For once, everything in the lighthouse was completely boring and normal.

Connie and I both let out a long breath. "I guess Snuffles didn't leave you those messages after all," Connie said. "Sorry, Snuffles," she said to the air. "I'm sure your spelling is very good."

Like Pop-Pop said, all experiments needed to be repeated, but for now, it seemed to me that Snuffles wasn't much of a writer.

"I'd bet money on the messages being from Lucas," I said.

"And your toy car?"

"Short-circuit."

Connie laughed at that. "You have answers for everything."

"Almost everything," I said, thinking about how I hardly had any answers at all. I was trying to sound more confident than I actually was. I wasn't sure of anything when it came to Connie or Spectacle Key.

Downstairs, we heard Papi start yelling about the ice maker in the refrigerator churning out black ice.

We listened to him for a while before Connie said, "I know you're trying to find explanations for what's going on here. But I think there's something very wrong with Spectacle Key. If I'm part of that, I've got to try to make it right again."

Her words felt like a hug. I hadn't wanted to admit the ways that the scientific method was letting me down, or that

I really had no idea why so many strange things were happening on the island. But it was good to be on a team for once, to try to solve a problem with a friend and not all on my own.

Downstairs, Mom was yelling, "NOW WHAT?!"

Frustrated that my parents were fighting *again*, I got up and kicked the foot of my bed hard. Pain shot up my leg. "Ow!" I growled, then sat back down on my bed with a thump.

"Maybe we can fix this," Connie said. "That memory of my momma? It was a happy remembrance, even though it made me sad. I know that doesn't make sense. But she was smiling at me in it. I want to see your parents smiling, too. I want that for you, Frank."

I was too choked up to say anything, so I just nodded.

Downstairs, we each grabbed a box of to-go cereal and a protein shake from the fridge. I packed more snacks and drinks and a bag of gummy bears into my duffel bag, just in case. Mary Shelley scarfed down her kibble and was ready in a flash.

"Breakfast on the go. The best modern invention!" I said to Connie once we got outside.

Connie took a sip of the shake and her lips twisted in a scowl. "Ugh. I don't know about that!"

We tromped across the island with Mary Shelley running ahead as always and waking up the dragonflies. Halfway there I started noticing signs. They'd been staked into the ground every few feet. They read:

LIGHTHOUSE HABITATION
ZONING MEETING
ALL KEYS RESIDENTS INVITED
TOMORROW AT 4 P.M.
PROTECT SPECTACLE KEY'S
HISTORICAL SIGNIFICANCE
—HAUNT

I plucked one out of the ground. "Tomorrow? I don't think Mom and Papi know about it."

"That Ms. Shiverton is very stubborn," Connie said. "Maybe she spends too much time on Spectacle Key. This place does seem to make adults a little grumpy."

Some people don't need a curse to be nasty. They just are, I thought, though I didn't say anything.

We finally reached the house and stopped before going in. "Do you remember anything about this place?" I asked Connie.

She shook her head. "Not a thing. But my stomach hurts and I don't think it has anything to do with your 'breakfast on the go.'"

"There has to be a reason why you came back here. Let's see if we can find anything out." I led the way through one of the arches to the cooler interior of the building. It was as sandy and smelly as ever, but now I started noticing things I hadn't before. Where the sand had blown away, we could see more of the tiled floor. I cleared some sand

and unveiled the letters *I F H* in blue tile right in the center of the room.

"Look at this," I said, kneeling down.

Connie knelt beside me. "I wonder what the letters stand for." Connie put her hand on the tiles and closed her eyes. "Frank!" she shouted at once. "I remember something about this place." Connie outlined the tiles with her fingertip and closed her eyes. "I can see it just like it was yesterday—lots of feet standing in a circle around the letters. There's singing. I think . . . I think it's the national anthem!" Connie jumped up and started scanning what was left of the roof. "There!" she said, running to a nearby wall. "See those hooks, Frank? They held up a flag once."

"Was this a military base or something?" I wondered.

Connie shrugged. "Just feet, a song, and a flag. That's all I remember."

"That's awesome, though," I said encouragingly, because Connie seemed disappointed in herself. "Maybe if we try another room you'll have more memories." I glanced around. The staircase! We hadn't checked out the upstairs yet. I ran toward it, with Mary Shelley bounding behind me.

"Stop!" cried Connie. "Not up there. It isn't safe. You could fall through the ceiling."

There were holes here and there overhead where the sky pierced through. "Maybe you have a point," I admitted. "Kitchen?"

Connie nodded. Mary Shelley beat us there and she sat and whined at something written in the sand.

THIS WAY, FARNK →

"It's the Mysterious Misspeller!" Connie whispered.

I raised an eyebrow at her. "Is that what we're calling them?"

"I'm good at names, Frank," she said like it was the most obvious thing in the world.

"You know, it's probably just Lucas and his pranks," I argued.

Connie pursed her lips. "Let's find out, then."

The arrow was pointing to a pantry door. I opened it slowly. The rusty hinges creaked. Broken shelves and empty jars formed a layer under our feet. At the back of the pantry hung a large sheet of burlap. I pushed it aside and found a glass doorknob. Another door! I tried turning it, but it wouldn't budge.

The sound of sniffing filled the tight room.

"Snuffles is here, too!" Connie said, clapping.

First the Mysterious Misspeller and now Snuffles? We were surrounded by possible ghosts! Then there was Connie. I still didn't like thinking of her as a ghost. A shiver shook me from top to bottom at the thought of being the only *alive* person in the room.

I twisted the knob with both hands and rammed my shoulder into the door. Still it wouldn't open.

"Now what?" I asked.

I half expected Lucas to come out and yell, "Gotcha!" Mary Shelley had crowded into the pantry, too. She bit down on the burlap that covered the door and pulled until it came away.

"Look, Frank!" Connie said, and gripped my arm in terror.

Sniff, went Snuffles.

A slow, red, vertical line was forming on the door.

"Is it blood?" Connie asked in a hushed voice.

I put out a trembling finger and touched the wet line, which was now curving into a familiar shape. It was sticky and when I smelled it, the red stuff had a sweet scent.

"No, I think it's some kind of jelly." The line curved into an *S*.

Then a *P*, an *E*, another *E*, a *K*, and soon, an entire sentence appeared in what must have been strawberry jam.

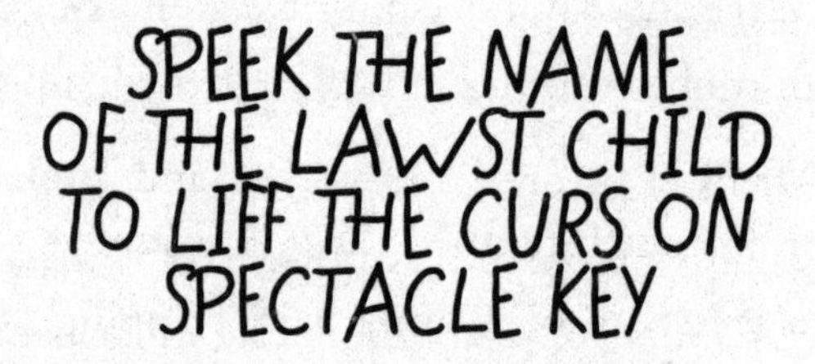

Everything was very silent then except for Mary Shelley's panting.

"Do you still think this is Lucas's prank?" Connie asked.

I shook my head. There was no way Lucas, or any human for that matter, was behind this. "We were right. This island is totally cursed," I said. The Mysterious Misspeller was telling us how to fix it, but I wanted to know *why* it was cursed in the first place. Scientists always need to know why a thing isn't working before they can safely propose a solution. I was certain that the curse could only be broken if we understood why it started.

"What happens if we do what it says?" inquired Connie. "Will the door open? Is it a magic door?"

My whole body was shaking as I reached out and tried the glass doorknob again. Still stuck.

"The Mysterious Misspeller is trying to help," Connie said.

I agreed. "'Speak the name of the lost child,'" I read out loud. "What do you think? Is that you, Connie? Are you the lost child?"

Snuffles sniffed loudly.

"Snuffles seems to think so," Connie said. "And I suppose I am very, very lost."

"Okay then." I cleared my throat and spoke Connie's name very loudly. "Connie Friday!"

Nothing happened. The door was still closed, and the doorknob wouldn't turn.

"We should try my full name," Connie said.

I snapped my fingers. "Yes, makes sense." I took a deep breath and said, "Zirconium Friday!"

Again, nothing.

"If it's not me, then who can it be?" Connie asked. She slumped against Mary Shelley, thinking.

The heat in the pantry was making it hard to breathe. "I need some air," I said, and left Connie and Mary Shelley behind. I walked past the archway and back outside and I didn't stop until I reached the stony beach. A rock jutted out a bit over the water, and I sat down on it.

A sniff tickled my ear.

"Leave me alone, Snuffles. And tell the Mysterious Misspeller to leave better clues while you're at it."

That earned me a snort so loud that my eardrum rang for a while. I tensed up, afraid that Snuffles was more than just irritated, but eventually, they went away. How many spirits were on this island, anyway? I regretted the thought at once. What if there were hundreds? Thousands? The idea of it made me feel weak, like I might topple into the ocean and drift away.

For now it was just me and the sea, the sky bright and clear, and the dragonflies that flitted close, then zoomed off. *I don't think I'm smart enough to figure this out,* I thought gloomily. Connie was the lost child. She *had* to be. And there was something hidden beyond that door that might help her figure out who she was, and maybe lift the curse on Spectacle Key.

Now I *was* sure it was a curse. Something bad had happened in that abandoned building. I could feel it—a lonely feeling. I knew about being lonely. Year in and out, I'd sit at school all by myself. As soon as I thought I'd made a friend, my parents would announce that we were moving again, into an old church or a water tower or something.

A seagull landed on a rock nearby and squawked. Again

and again it screeched at the sky. "Can't find your flock?" I asked, but at the sound of my voice the bird took off.

Maybe it was lost and lonely. A little like me.

Lost. A lost child.

Could the Mysterious Misspeller have meant . . . me?

I jumped off the rock and ran back to the ruin. Connie and Mary Shelley were still in the pantry and Connie was saying a bunch of random names.

"Jenny! Ophelia! Ann! Marie! Matilda! Rose! Jane!"

"What are you doing?" I shouted over her.

"Margaret! Elizab— Oh. Hello, Frank. Just trying out some names that I had in my head. I thought maybe one of them might belong to me. So far nothing's worked," she said, jiggling the doorknob.

"Let me try," I said. My voice was a little shaky. I coughed, swallowed hard, then said, "Francisco Fernández Jr.!"

My hands were tingling as I reached out to turn the doorknob. I counted in my head, *one, two, three . . .*

But the door remained firmly stuck.

"You aren't lost, Frank," Connie said. Her mouth was turned down in the corners. "You just need a friend. But you've got me now."

"Thanks, Connie," I said. Mary Shelley licked my hand, too, and I gave her head a good rub. We spent the rest of the day in the abandoned house, trying out names that sounded like they were from 1921, giving up only when Connie shouted, "EBENEZER SCROOGE!" at the door and gave it a giant kick. In the corner of the pantry she discovered a broken-in-half broom, and we used it to sweep the sand off the floor in the foyer, uncovering the circular mosaic with *I F H* written on it. She swept away the messages from the Mysterious Misspeller, humming her lullaby all the while.

I'd packed extra granola bars in my duffel bag, plus two sodas. We ate and drank on the mosaic and wondered what had happened to the building.

"A storm, I'm guessing," Connie said, chewing thoughtfully.

"A big one," I added. The sunshine poured in through the broken windows of the building and the places where the wall was crumbling.

Connie traced the letters *I F H*. "Tornadoes sound like trains," she said. "I don't know how I know that, but I do."

Snuffles sniffed all around us then. At the sound, Mary Shelley started barking, snapping her jaws in the air.

"Leave Snuffles alone," I said, patting the floor so Mary Shelley would come sit by me. She gave me a dirty look but sat down anyway.

"Good dog," Connie said, and gave Mary Shelley a kiss.

Outside, the wind was picking up again and clouds were darkening the sky. "We'd better go," I said, and started packing up what was left of our snacks.

Before stepping outside, Connie looked in the direction of the locked door, cupped her hands around her mouth, and yelled, "GEORGIA FINKEL!"

I listened for the creaking of the door, but there was only the wind.

"Worth a try," Connie said.

"Was that just some random name?" I asked.

Connie shook her head. "A girl I knew. She was always picking her nose." Connie made an 'ew' face.

I grabbed Connie's arm to stop her from walking. "A girl you knew? You remembered something else!"

Gasping, Connie wrapped her arms around me and gave me a hug. "Good old Georgia Finkel! She could jump rope better than anybody. That's my memory—of a girl jumping rope with her finger up her nose!"

We laughed all the way to the lighthouse. Remembering Georgia Finkel wasn't really helpful, but it lifted our spirits. Even Snuffles sniffed the whole time. They sounded like happy sniffs to me, but then again, what did I know?

Chapter 16

THE TROUBLE WITH FAIRY TALES

There was something different about the lighthouse as we approached. It seemed to be moving somehow, wiggling against the sky. Connie, Mary Shelley, and I slowed down. Were my eyes playing tricks on me? My heart filled with dread. My parents were inside! I started to run. What if the lighthouse was about to walk into the sea with them? "Mom! Papi!" I screamed.

"Slow down, Frank!" Connie cried behind me. But I was speeding now, the lighthouse coming fully into view. The closer I got, the more I saw. The lighthouse wasn't moving—what was ON it was moving! That's when I stopped. The bright white stone that made up the exterior was covered in thick, pale vines. And the vines were crawling up the walls and growing before our eyes. Pink flowers sprouted at the ends of the vines like trumpets, and bees buzzed around the flowers, dipping in to get a drink and then zipping off again. The vines grew tendrils and shoots as we watched, making the building look as if it were taking a breath. One by one, thick thorns grew out of the vines, until the lighthouse was covered in spikes.

"It's like a fairy tale!" Connie said.

"Looks like Spectacle Key strikes again," I responded.

My parents were standing outside, staring speechlessly at the lighthouse. Mom had her hands on her head, while Papi looked like he was hyperventilating.

"What's going on?" I asked them.

Mom threw her hands in the air. "Who knows? One minute, we were working on the lamp on the top floor when we heard a tapping on the glass. So we looked up and it was a vine, knocking on the lighthouse in the breeze."

"The next thing we knew, these vines had sprung up out of nowhere. Look at the roots on these things, Junior!" Papi said, holding up what looked like a potato.

"I always knew Florida had wild ecology, but this is completely bonkers," Mom said.

"We'd better get to work," Papi added, handing Mom a spade.

"Mister, why don't you go inside and get your dinner. It's warm on the stove," Mom told me as she started hacking away at a vine near the front door.

Inside, I stopped and rubbed my face, exhausted. We'd

spent almost the whole day at the abandoned building and hadn't come any closer to figuring out what was wrong with Spectacle Key, or where Connie had come from. Now super-fast-growing, thorn-covered vines were trying to take over the lighthouse? Maybe it was time to call it quits.

"It could be worse," Connie said beside me.

"How so?"

"They're just plants, Frank. Could've been snakes!"

Snuffles made a long snorting sound.

"I guess Snuffles agrees with you," I said. "Come on, let's grab dinner and then go upstairs. We can try more names if you'd like."

In the kitchen, a still-warm plate of arroz con pollo sat in the microwave. I picked out two forks and sat down at the table across from Connie.

"Smells good," she said.

"It's Papi's specialty," I told her, then we dug in. I ate my half and Connie "ate" hers.

Outside, my parents yanked and cursed at the vines that continued to twirl up the lighthouse. Every so often, one of them would yell, "Ouch!" when a thorn pricked them. Connie watched them through the kitchen window. "Oh no," she said after a while.

I got up to look. I couldn't hear them, but my parents were definitely fighting again. Mom's hands were on her hips and Papi was pointing a finger at her. Both of them were yelling at each other and neither one was listening.

"I hate this so much," I said.

Connie had drifted over to a bookshelf in the living room. She was holding my parents' wedding portrait. They'd gotten married on the beach, and in the photograph, they were barefoot, and the wind was picking up Mom's veil so that it looked like a cloud in the sky. Papi had the biggest smile.

"It's the curse, Frank," Connie said. "We have to find a way to lift it. Maybe if we can figure out the name of the lost child—my name, my *real* name—then everything will be better."

"I hope so," I said, and began to wash my dirty dishes, keeping my eyes away from the window. I was tired of seeing Mom and Papi fight. Besides, the vines were nearly blocking the view. When I finished, I saw Connie waiting for me at the stairs. She was holding a book with a blue cover.

"Fairy tales! There are curses in nearly all these stories," she said with a knowing look in her eyes.

"The trouble with fairy tales is that they aren't real," I said.

"Neither are ghosts."

"If you say so," I said, and followed her up the stairs to my room. Mary Shelley whined at Bernard up on the windowsill, so I let her take the doll to her bed. Then Connie and I thumbed through the book of fairy tales.

"Let's see. Snow White was cursed with a poisoned apple," Connie said.

"No longer eating apples on Spectacle Key. Check," I said.

Connie giggled and flipped through the book some more.

"Lots of people get turned into animals in these stories. Frogs, bears, that sort of thing."

"I wouldn't mind being a bear," I said, thinking of Florida black bears that could knock down trees just by leaning on them.

Snuffles sniffed along as Connie talked, their sniffs getting louder and louder. I wondered if they were allergic to something in my room. Maybe it was the vines. Outside, the plants were just beginning to reach my window and they tapped the glass, just like Mom and Papi had said.

"Ooh! There's the story of the twelve dancing princesses," Connie said. Her face shone brighter than lamplight as she spoke. I got the feeling she was just reading the stories for fun now.

"What? Were they cursed with dancing?" I asked, rolling my eyes.

"Exactly!" Connie said.

Snuffles sniffed some more at that.

"Any stories about runny noses?" I asked, and we both laughed.

That's when Mary Shelley started to growl, low and long, hovering over Bernard like it was her puppy. "What's wrong, girl?" I asked.

Suddenly the fairy tale book flew out of Connie's hands and sailed across the room, slamming against the door. Connie yelped in surprise.

Sniff!

"What the—" I started to say, but the lamps toppled off my nightstands, crashing into smithereens on the floor and plunging the room into darkness.

Sniff!

An unseen hand wrenched Bernard away from Mary Shelley, and she barked and growled, baring all her teeth. I'd never seen her so mad. Meanwhile, Bernard floated in midair, its button eyes staring directly at us.

"Make it stop!" Connie was saying. She'd grabbed my pillow and was hugging it with all her might.

"Okay, okay," I said. My heart felt like it was going to burst out of my chest. If there was a monster in my room, I didn't know if I could do anything to stop it. Bernard was very still in the air. Slobbery dog toy or not, Bernard was one messed up and haunted doll.

Just as I was about to grab Bernard, its head started to spin! It started out slowly, as if Bernard was trying to get a careful, 360-degree view of my room, but then sped up so fast that the key around its neck whizzed like a knife through the air and one of the doll's black shoes came off. Mary Shelley whined and covered her head with her paws. I jumped back onto the bed and hugged Connie and her pillow. I drew the line at head-spinning dolls. What if Bernard had teeth? I'd never even considered that!

SNIFF SNIFF SNIFF, went Snuffles.

Outside, the vines thumped against the glass so hard that a hairline crack appeared in my window.

SNIIIIIIFFFFFFFFFFFFFFF! SNNNNNNNIIIIIFFFFFF!

"Now's not the time for an allergy attack, Snuffles!" I shouted.

The paper and pen I'd left on my bed earlier suddenly rose in the air. The words appeared quickly, the pen punching through the paper every so often:

"It's Snuffles! Snuffles is doing all of this!" Connie screamed.

As soon as she said it, the vines retreated from my window, and Bernard fell to the ground with a thud.

We were quiet, though our breaths were loud and ragged.

I felt so stupid. There was no Mysterious Misspeller. Snuffles had been trying to communicate with us all along. Suddenly, I realized what Ms. McCartney had meant by giving me the magnifying glass with the words *Read between the lines* etched on it. I hadn't given Snuffles enough careful thought. I thought I could command Snuffles to write something, and when they didn't, that was all the proof I needed.

I hadn't tried to figure out the *feelings* behind the sniffles. Maybe Snuffles only communicated when they were angry, or sad. Maybe Snuffles had been toying with us.

"Snuffles, what are you?" I whispered at last, my voice trembling and my legs shaking so hard I wasn't sure I could walk.

On the cracked window, words slowly appeared, etched into the glass and making a sound ten times worse than nails on a chalkboard.

NOT WHAT, FARNK. WHO

Chapter 17

SCARE

You can't blame us for not wanting to stay in my room after that. Connie and I jumped off my bed and headed for the door. Mary Shelley was right behind us, Bernard back in her mouth.

"Oh no you don't," I said, snatching the doll and throwing it into my room.

"It'll follow us anyway," Connie said, and then shook all over.

"Bernard isn't the problem. It's been Snuffles this whole time. And Snuffles just turned my room into the set of a horror movie." I'd read a ton of scary books, but nothing compared to the real thing. In the books, the main characters always figured out what to do. But this wasn't a book. This was my weird and suddenly haunted life! And what I wanted more than anything was my mom and papi. I didn't care if that made me sound like a baby. It was the truth.

"Why didn't Snuffles write on the paper earlier, when we asked them to?" Connie asked.

I shook my head. "I don't know. It's not like poltergeists are known for following directions when asked nicely."

Inside my room, something fell to the floor with a thud. More thuds followed. I was pretty sure Snuffles was knocking all my books down. *My books!* Anger grew hot in my chest, but there was nothing I could do about it.

"Poltergeists?" Connie asked.

I'd seen a really scary movie about poltergeists once and hadn't been able to sleep alone in my room for a week. But what we'd just seen made the movie look like a cartoon. "Poltergeists are ghosts that are known for moving things around, causing a mess, sometimes hurting people."

"So Snuffles is a ghost? Like me?" Connie said in a small voice.

"Not like you," I told her. Snuffles wasn't anything like Connie. But if I had to make a hypothesis, then I'd guess that, yes, Snuffles was a spirit, too. An angry one.

"No, not exactly. I don't have tantrums," Connie added.

"Yeah. Snuffles is having one massive tantrum right now," I whispered. "So maybe we need to give them some room."

I went downstairs, followed by Connie and Mary Shelley.

"I wonder why Snuffles is having a tantrum," Connie asked out loud. "That's the thing we need to figure out."

The truth was, I was fed up with mysteries that just

seemed to pile on top of one another. I sighed. "Yep. Another mystery, I guess."

Connie was pacing in the kitchen, back and forth, making me dizzy. "We're so close, Frank. I can almost taste the answers."

Outside, my parents were still hacking away at the vines that Snuffles had sent to attack the lighthouse. The green tendrils were limp and didn't seem to be growing anymore. Maybe Snuffles's tantrum was over.

My parents looked exhausted.

I felt exhausted suddenly.

"Maybe we can take a break, Connie. Like, go help Mom and Papi with the plant problem. Get our minds off the curse and all the weird stuff?"

Connie stared at me, her mouth open. Then her eyebrows tightened, like she was upset with me. "Take a break? Frank Fernández, I'm disappointed in y—"

I didn't let her finish. Maybe ghosts didn't get overwhelmed. Maybe they didn't lose hope. But that's how I was feeling now. *Connie just doesn't get it,* I thought. So instead of talking with her, I went outside. "Can I help?" I asked my parents.

"Heads up, Junior," Papi said, tossing a pair of gardening gloves at me. I put them on and grabbed some gardening shears.

Beside me, Connie was anxiously gripping the hem of the T-shirt she wore, pacing back and forth. "We need to go back to the abandoned house. We need to find my name. Frank, this isn't the time for gardening. We're partners, remember?"

"Just shut up, okay?" I whispered. My eyes stung. I didn't want to deal with Connie, or Snuffles, or creepy dolls and curses. I just wanted to hang out with my parents, get sweaty clearing away the vines, eat dinner, read a book, and go to bed. Though I wasn't sure I wanted to sleep in my room ever again.

My hands shook so much I couldn't hang on to the shears. I kept dropping them.

Connie got in front of me, her arms crossed and brow furrowed. "Frank, we have to solve this mystery!"

My chest felt all tight and funny, the way it always did when my parents would announce that we were moving again. The feeling bloomed in my chest like a little sun, heating me up from the inside. If I didn't say something, I'd burn up.

"Go away!" I shouted, unable to stop myself.

Connie gasped. My parents looked over to where I was, and I guess they assumed I was talking to the vines, because they went on with their work.

"Do you mean it, Frank?" Connie asked.

I hated myself. I hated every single bit of myself in that moment. But still, I said, "Yes."

In an instant, Connie vanished. She didn't even make a sound. She was just . . . gone. I rubbed my eyes and whispered her name, panic rising in my chest by the second.

Then I burst into tears.

"Oh, mister, mister, it's okay," Mom said, rushing over to where I was standing, the gardening shears dangling from my hand.

Papi was there, too, pulling me into a hug. "Vamos, Junior, it's not so bad. They're just plants."

For some reason, that made me cry even harder.

So we took a break inside. Papi said, "Let's make popcorn and watch a movie. The vines can wait. This whole lighthouse can just wait." I almost started crying again, this time in relief. Ever since we'd moved to Spectacle Key, every single day had been work, work, work. Move in the boxes, unpack them, fix the broken things, fix more broken things, sweep out the dead bugs and lizards, discover ghosts, and on and on. Nothing sounded better than a movie and popcorn.

There was a persistent thought in the back of my mind, though, one buzzing like a mosquito.

Connie. I'd made her disappear.

My only friend was now gone. I bit my lip and tried not to cry again. *I'm sorry, Connie. Come back,* I thought over and over again.

"Scoot over," Mom said, and squeezed next to me on the couch. She'd put a movie into the DVD player. It was an old black-and-white film Pop-Pop had bought for us—*I Was a Teenage Frankenstein*. The box described it like this: *Body of a Boy! Mind of a Monster!* I'd seen it a million times. In this version of the Frankenstein story, Dr. Frankenstein had an alligator hidden in a pit underneath his laboratory. It was silly and scary and a perfect distraction.

Except, all through the movie, I couldn't stop thinking about Connie. I didn't mean to make her go away. I just hadn't wanted to face my problems. Like the monster in the movie—I meant well, but I'd ruined everything.

The movie was almost over, and the bowl of popcorn only had a few kernels left in it. Papi was snoring on the couch and Mom's eyes were closed, too. Mary Shelley was lying down in the kitchen, out like a light. If Connie were here, she'd be watching the movie with me. I wondered if she'd be afraid of the gruesome parts, or if she'd think the dialogue was funny. Suddenly I felt really alone, more alone than I'd ever been before.

I remembered how she'd said she'd never even seen a movie. Poor Connie. What had I done?

"Connie, please come back," I whispered out loud.

That's when I heard a knock on the door.

Connie! I thought. I ran to the door and yanked it open. But Connie wasn't there. Instead, it was Ms. Shiverton and someone I'd never seen before. He was a tall and skinny white man. His hair was long and gray and tied back in a ponytail. He wore socks with his sandals.

"Are your parents home?" Ms. Shiverton asked. Her HAUNT badge was crooked on her pink blouse.

"Yeah," I said, and went back into the lighthouse. I woke up my parents, who stood, stretched blearily, and went outside.

The man in socks and sandals introduced himself. "My name is Gregory, but you can call me Buzz."

"Buzz?" Papi repeated, stifling another yawn. My parents were really tired.

Buzz nodded. "Yep. I own an apiary on Hibiscus Key. Best bees and honey in the country! Hence, Buzz. Get it?"

"We got it," Mom said. "How can we help you, Buzz?"

Ms. Shiverton cleared her throat. "Gregory is the president of SCARE. That's the Society for the Care of At-Risk Environments." Ms. Shiverton smiled without showing her teeth.

"You're kidding," I said.

"Never," Ms. Shiverton replied.

Buzz reached out to touch one of the vines that had grown over the lighthouse. "Ah," he crooned, rubbing the leaf gently. "This is passion coral vine. Very rare."

Ms. Shiverton joined him. "Very rare, you say?"

Buzz nodded, half paying attention and mumbling about "passion coral vine honey, mmm . . ."

I watched Mom and Papi carefully. They'd shaken off their sleepiness and were on high alert.

"Rare or not, it's a nuisance. It's absolutely taken over our house!" Mom said.

Ms. Shiverton gasped as if she'd just heard the most shocking thing. "Firstly, it's a lighthouse, not your house. I just happened to be in the neighborhood and saw you and your husband doing some fairly aggressive pruning. We must treat the rare flora and fauna of Spectacle Key with respect. Isn't that right, Gregory?"

"Buzz, please," Buzz said, taking a whiff of one of the passion coral vine flowers.

"Now I have been very patient with you, Mr. and Mrs. Fernández—" Ms. Shiverton began.

"Bless your heart," Mom interrupted, and I held my breath. Whenever Mom said, "Bless your heart," I knew she meant the very opposite.

Emily Shiverton took a step backward. Maybe she spoke Southern, too.

"What my wife means to say is—" Papi started.

Mom took a giant step toward Ms. Shiverton. "What I mean to say, and I don't need an interpreter, Francisco, thank you very much, is that you and your nosy, interloping, busybody HAUNT minions couldn't drag me out of this lighthouse with a team of thoroughbreds. In fact, I'd like to see you try."

Papi beamed, brighter than any lighthouse lamp could ever glow. "You tell her, Joyce," he said.

"I just did," Mom said without taking her eyes off Ms. Shiverton.

With that, the vines started to move again. Slowly, one of them crept along the ground, getting closer and closer to Ms. Shiverton.

Suddenly, a thought struck me. What if Snuffles was on HAUNT's side? What if Snuffles wanted us to leave Spectacle Key, too? But it wasn't a question I could just ask Snuffles, was it? If I asked, "So, Snuffles, are you evil?" I might not like the answer, or worse, I could set off another horrifying tantrum.

Ms. Shiverton didn't seem to notice the vine. And she

didn't seem too bothered by my Mom's outburst. Instead, she turned to Buzz and said, "Don't you think the Fernándezes should depart the island so that SCARE can conduct a survey of this rare environment?"

"BUT LOOK AT THEM!" Papi said as a vine began wrapping itself around Ms. Shiverton's ankle. She glanced at it and shook it off, stomping the vine with her heel.

"I don't know about all that," Buzz said at last. "Sometimes a little bit of pruning helps. And I sure would like a cutting or two to grow over on my key."

"Think of the bees!" Ms. Shiverton urged.

Buzz frowned. The vines wiggled like snakes. "These really are quick growers! Perhaps a survey would be helpful."

"Snuffles," I whispered, "please stop. I'll help you, I promise," I said under my breath.

With that, the vines began to retreat.

"Will you look at that!" Buzz said. He snapped off a few tendrils and pocketed them. "Prune a bit here and there," he started to say, and Papi followed Buzz around the lighthouse, getting a quick lesson in rare-vine maintenance. Meanwhile, Ms. Shiverton and my mom glared at one another with narrowed eyes.

Finally, Ms. Shiverton said, "The mayor will be in touch soon."

"I'm looking forward to it," Mom answered her.

Chapter 18

APOLOGIES

After everything that had happened in my room, I didn't really want to sleep there, especially now that Connie was gone.

Gone, because I'd told her to go.

So I asked Mom and Papi if I could sleep with them because I was scared that Snuffles would do something again, and because I was trying to get Connie off my mind.

Papi looked at me funny. "Junior, you haven't done this in a while," he said, but still, he scooted over to make room for me between him and Mom.

Mom ruffled my hair and turned off the lights. She trailed her hand up and down my arm for a while, like she used to when I was little and would run into their bedroom after a nightmare. Back then, sleeping with my folks was a habit. I hated feeling so lonely in my room, and I felt safe with my parents. But it meant they didn't get much sleep, so Mom and Papi tried everything to get me to stop. They bribed me with toys, punished me with time-outs, even bought me a hamster to keep me company. The hamster was named Olaf, and he made such a racket all night long on his wheel that he kept *all* of us up.

Nothing worked until I read my first monster book, and something in my brain went *click*. I figured, if the monsters lived in books, then they couldn't get me.

But all that changed when Snuffles decided to go berserk in my bedroom.

Settling in with Mom and Papi made me feel like I was seven again, except back then, I knew everything would be all right and nothing could hurt me. Things were different now. I couldn't sleep anyway. Papi started snoring and Mom slept like an armadillo—rolled up and squeezing me in next to Papi. Besides all that, my brain was being very unkind to me, reliving the moment when I told Connie to go, again and again, on a horrible loop.

Stop it, brain, I said to myself, but it didn't work. There's something really terrible about thinking in the middle of the night. You just think and think and never come up with a plan. It wasn't until the sun rose through my parents' bedroom that I finally realized I could try to do something about Connie. I could attempt the experiment again. Maybe that would bring her back!

Bleary-eyed, my parents and I got out of bed and headed

to the kitchen for breakfast. The windows were clear and free of vines. We ran outside into a deep fog and saw that the plants that had smothered the lighthouse yesterday had disappeared altogether. While Mom and Papi counted their blessings, I worried that Snuffles was only gearing up to do something far worse to us. I'd promised to help. What if I couldn't keep my word? What was Snuffles capable of?

One problem at a time, I told myself. First I planned to re-create the exothermic reaction that brought Connie out in the first place. Patting my pocket, I made sure I had gummy bears with me, too. Red ones. Scientists always had to make sure that every detail was the same when replicating an experiment. I ate a quick breakfast, then went upstairs to pack up my chemistry set. When we reached the door, Mary Shelley refused to enter my room. "I know, girl. Gives me the creeps, too," I said. She whined from the hall as I got dressed. I wondered if she also missed Connie.

Outside, the fog still sat like a blanket on the ground. Mary Shelley stayed close by as we made our way to the ruin. I karate-chopped the air, pretending I was cutting through the fog. It was like walking with my eyes closed, and soon, the arches of the abandoned house were right in front of me.

"Here goes nothing," I said to Mary Shelley. The mosaic was sand-covered again, and all the notes that Snuffles, aka the Mysterious Misspeller, had left were gone, too. I rushed over to the door inside the pantry and even the red message about the lost child had disappeared.

It was like everything had gone quiet. The vines, Snuffles, Connie, the messages—all the evidence of what I'd seen and experienced in the last few days had vanished! For a moment, I felt a rush of relief. Was it all over? Would Mom, Papi, Mary Shelley, and I get to live on Spectacle Key in peace? Maybe Mom was right. Maybe I really did suffer from heatstroke!

"Connie?" I called. Only the wind whistling through the building answered. In the distance, I heard seagulls squawking, and beyond that, a truck blasting its horn on US 1. "Snuffles? Are you going to be nice today?" I asked next. My voice echoed a little.

That's when the scratching sound began, accompanied by a familiar sweet smell.

"Snuffles?" Terror rippled through my body and I held myself very still. A scraping sound started up behind me. Slowly, I turned around until I noticed an invisible finger drawing an arrow in the sand on the floor. It was pointing at the staircase. Connie had warned me about going upstairs. After all, the ceiling was basically Swiss cheese.

Maybe Snuffles was leading me to my death—or maybe they wanted me to figure out what happened on Spectacle Key. The moment I started toward the staircase, Mary Shelley whimpered.

"I know," I said to my dog. "But I did promise to help Snuffles." I placed my foot on the first step, then the second. "It'll hold me, I think," I said out loud, more for myself than for my dog.

Cautiously, I took the third step, then the fourth. The iron handrail was rusty, and when I touched it, the metal came away in big orange flakes. And that's when my left leg plunged through the rotten wood. Mary Shelley barked and spun around. "I'm fine!" I shouted at her, tugging myself out of the hole I'd made, but she howled until I was free. I wished I had a Great Dane translator. She was probably saying, *I tried to warn you, Frank.* There were three more steps to go.

Taking a huge breath, I ran up the remaining steps. The wood groaned as if the whole place was angry at me. Below, Mary Shelley stood on her hind legs and whined. "I'll be right back!" I shouted.

I was standing before a dark hallway. On either side of the hall were several closed doors. The letters *I F H* were painted on each one. Where should I start?

"Now what, Snuffles?"

All on its own, the door to my left creaked open.

My heart pounded so hard I was sure that Mary Shelley could hear it downstairs. I rubbed my hands together, waiting for the door to stop moving. When it was finally still, I started forward, then thought better of it. What if Snuffles locked me in? Would I be able to jump from the window?

A sniff echoed in the hall. "Is that supposed to be an encouraging sound or a threatening one?" I asked out loud. Snuffles sniffed again. "Okay, well. That explains nothing," I said, and entered the room in one brave stride.

The room was brightly lit with sunshine. Faded, flowery

wallpaper hung in strips here and there. A broken crib leaned against one wall and a rusty bedframe under the window. Glass crunched underfoot. Lying on its side in the center of the room was a chest with all its drawers open and empty except for a baby bottle packed with sand. There was a big mirror on the floor, too, the kind that had once stood up on four legs and tilted back and forth. A long crack like a lightning bolt had appeared in it. In another corner was a single brown boot. The laces had mostly disintegrated, but I could tell that they'd once been red.

Red like the laces on Connie's boots.

"Connie," I whispered. I went to pick up the boot, my fingers trembling, when I saw something moving out of the corner of my eye.

The mirror. Maybe it was just sunlight reflecting off the glass. I leaned over to take a good look at it, wondering what face had last peered at themselves in it. That's when I saw a pair of brown eyes and a freckly face reflected back at me

Downstairs, Mary Shelley howled, long and sad.

I whipped around to find Connie standing there, hugging herself. She was still wearing my alligator T-shirt, but she had the look of someone who had just seen something terrible.

"Connie? Is it really you?"

Connie nodded.

"Yes!" I shouted. "You're back! I was worried you'd be gone forever. I'm so sorry, Connie. I never want you to go away. Never ever, okay?" I was saying excitedly, but Connie just stood there with her arms wrapped around herself.

I stopped and took a deep breath. Maybe Connie wasn't ready to forgive me. I could've kicked myself. What was the right way to apologize and make her know I meant it?

"I really didn't mean what I said," I whispered. "How can I make things okay again?"

Connie closed her eyes and unwrapped her arms from around herself. Then she held up her hands for me to see.

I gasped. Her hands weren't solid anymore. I could see through them and they flickered on and off that way, as if they were on a bad circuit or something.

"Frank," Connie said at last, her voice squeaky as she held back tears, "what's happening to me?"

Chapter 19

WHISPERS IN A SUDDEN STORM

Connie hid her hands in the pockets of her dress.

"Does it hurt?" I asked quietly.

Connie shook her head. "It doesn't even tingle. But I don't want to fade away altogether. Do you think I will, Frank? It's bad enough that only you can see me."

"I don't know," I said. Why would Connie be slowly disappearing *now*?

Downstairs, Mary Shelley began to growl and bark. She was a pretty laid-back dog, so I rarely heard her growling. The sound made the hairs on the back of my neck stand up.

"We might not be alone," I said.

"Could it be Snuffles again?" Connie asked, her eyes wide in terror. Snuffles had scared us both out of our socks just the day before in my bedroom. I didn't blame Connie for being frightened, but I played it off.

"Who knows? It's Spectacle Key. Could be anybody. Aliens. Werewolves."

"Don't joke, Frank. Let's go downstairs and face it, whatever it is," Connie said.

"Together," I added, and the two of us left the room with the crib and baby bottle and a boot that looked just like Connie's. An idea had started to form in my head about Connie and the abandoned house, but it wasn't one I wanted to pay too much attention to just yet.

We managed the stairs really carefully, avoiding the jagged hole I'd made with my foot. The wood creaked and squealed at us, sounding like a bad violin lesson. The entire time, Mary Shelley had been growling in the direction of the kitchen. I felt Connie's hand on my arm when we finally reached the bottom floor. With a glance, I could see that it was still flickering in and out, disappearing at her wrist.

"Mary Shelley," I called softly, not wanting to draw attention to whatever it was that my dog had cornered in the kitchen. Dogs have a great sense of hearing, and at the sound of my voice she stopped snarling. I heard her paws padding over the sand as she returned to us, panting and drooling all over the place.

"What is it, pup?" Connie asked.

Mary Shelley only cocked her head to the side, then bolted into the kitchen.

"I guess she wants us to follow her," I said.

"Right!" Connie exclaimed, then took a deep breath and stood up straighter. "Into battle."

"When you put it that way," I said without finishing the sentence. I wasn't quite ready for a battle. Mainly, I was hoping Mary Shelley had just found a raccoon in the kitchen and not another one of Snuffle's messages or head-spinning dolls.

We slowly approached the kitchen. On the way, I grabbed a lamp covered in dry seaweed. It wasn't much of a weapon, and I wasn't sure it worked with invisible creatures like Snuffles, but I felt better holding it. Connie rolled her eyes at me, but we kept going.

"Hello?" I called, like every victim in every horror movie ever.

The pantry door was open, and inside, a shadow moved back and forth.

"This was a bad idea, Frank," Connie said, and started tugging me backward.

The shadow moved like liquid and the pantry door began to open wider. I closed my eyes tight as Connie wrapped her arms around me.

I heard feet crunching sand and then someone, or something, clearing their throat. I was pretty sure I was about to learn what it felt like to be digested alive.

That's when a voice boomed out, "Something terrible happened in this place. Can't you feel it?"

"Mama Z!" both Connie and I shouted at the same time.

We ran toward her—me, Connie, and Mary Shelley. My dog jumped up and set her big paws on Mama Z's shoulders.

"Siéntate," Mama Z commanded, and my dog did just that, sitting all prim and proper at Mama Z's feet.

"What are you doing here?" I asked.

"I had a dream last night," she whispered. "A nightmare about this place. In my dream, a sinkhole opened up beneath the building and swallowed it whole. It's a well-known fact that nightmares, if examined before breakfast, can never come true." Mama Z's stomach growled loudly. "And so I am here."

Connie and I both stared at the ground beneath our feet in terror. Sinkholes? Anything was possible on Spectacle Key.

Mama Z cleared her throat, then looked at me with narrowed eyes. "Is Connie Friday here?" she asked.

"Sí," I said, and pointed at Connie beside me. To Mama Z, it must have looked like I was pointing at thin air. Maybe, if Connie didn't stop flickering, thin air was all she would soon be. I held back a shiver.

"Good," Mama Z said. "Has she told you about what happened here?"

I looked at Connie, who only shrugged.

"We think it was a storm," I told Mama Z. "But Connie doesn't remember for sure."

"Not only a storm," Mama Z said, her voice low and gravelly. "Something else. Something far worse."

I thought about the things I'd seen upstairs and checked out Connie's boots with the red laces again. Yep. They were the same as the boot I'd found on the second floor.

Even though I was afraid of the answer, I still asked, "What happened?"

"I don't know. I can only sense the horror of it." Mama Z reached into the bag she wore slung across her body. Out of it she pulled a small crystal ball and held it in the palm of her hand.

"We don't have any money," I said.

Mama Z considered this for a moment, then she said, "Emergencies call for steep discounts. Let's say it's free of charge." Mama Z led the way into the main room of the house. She cleared sand off the mosaic with her foot, then she sat down, her skirts billowing around her. The crystal ball was set in the center of the mosaic. "Come, come," Mama Z told me. Connie and I joined her, while Mary Shelley settled down beside Mama Z.

All around us, the ruin was silent. I could hear the waves crashing against the shore nearby. Connie sat crisscross style beside me, her hands hidden in her dress again. Nearby, the duffel bag with my chemistry set inside lay on the floor. Part of me wondered how I'd even gotten here, sitting around a crystal ball instead of a science experiment.

"Now what?" I asked. "Do we close our eyes, hold hands, run for our lives?"

Mama Z smiled. "Simply, we begin with a question to

the witness of the long-ago horror that occurred in this place." Mama Z hummed and let her fingers flutter over the crystal ball.

"Connie is right here," I said. "We can just ask her. We don't need all"—I wiggled my fingers at the crystal ball—"this."

I could have sworn that Mama Z's nostrils flared at that, though she carried on as if I hadn't said a word. "Oh, witness," she called out in her big voice. "Do you feel compelled to speak today?"

I was about to repeat the question to Connie, just like I did the last time we had a séance with Mama Z. But before I could do that, we heard faint crying.

A child was crying somewhere. And sniffing a very familiar sniff.

"Do not weep; you are among friends," Mama Z thundered. She'd heard Snuffles! I wasn't suffering from heatstroke after all!

Snuffles blubbered some more.

"It's Snuffles!" Connie said. "And they're sad!"

Mama Z had grown very pale. Her hands on the crystal ball shook a little.

Snuffles cried harder. "I'm here. I'm here. Why didn't they come for me?" the small voice asked, as if very far away.

"Where are you now?" Mama Z asked.

The cries intensified into wails, choking and gasping for

air. "Help me, Frank!" Snuffles cried, and each time I heard it, my whole body went numb.

Just then, a bolt of lightning slammed into the sand outside the ruin, shaking the timbers around us and making our ears ring. Another, then another, lit up the ruin like a flashbulb. Each strike left an echo ringing in our ears, and beneath that was the sound of Snuffles wailing.

"Snuffles, stop! I don't know how to help you!" I yelled.

"Snuffles?" Mama Z asked, disbelief written all over her face.

Before I could explain, a bone-chilling scream ripped through the air as rain began to pour down.

"Tranquilo, tranquilo," Mama Z was saying, shushing Snuffles as if she were comforting a hurt child. Tears were streaming down her cheeks.

Snuffles stopped screaming and instead began to whisper. "Speak the name. Speak the name of the lost child." Lightning lit the world outside over and over again.

"We're trying. We don't know Connie's real name! And we don't know yours either!" I shouted over the whispers that wouldn't stop.

Connie was on her feet at this point, turning in circles and talking to the air. "I've named myself. Connie Friday. Isn't that enough?"

Snuffles started to cry again, asking, "I'm here. I'm here. Why didn't they come?"

"Why didn't WHO come?" Mama Z tried to get Snuffles to explain.

"NOT YOU!" Snuffles shrieked, and the crystal ball split in two.

Just as suddenly as it all began, the crying and screaming, the whispering, even the lightning stopped.

My stomach felt like it was doing flips inside me. "I might puke," I said out loud. Connie took one small step away from me, just in case I really did lose my breakfast.

Mama Z began to wrap the two halves of her broken crystal ball in a yellow scarf. Outside, rain pounded Spectacle Key.

"That's it?" I asked. "You just ask a bunch of questions, freaky stuff happens, and you pack up and go?"

"Impertinente," Mama Z muttered under her breath.

"Hey! I speak Spanish. A little," I said.

Mama Z carefully put the shattered ball into her bag. "There are many secrets on Spectacle Key," she said at last, an eyebrow raised as if the idea of those secrets irritated her. "Snuffles and Connie have chosen you to uncover them, Frank. They are the lost children of Spectacle Key and they have made themselves known to you and only you. I am clearly an intruder here. So what is Frank Fernández, the young keeper of the lighthouse, going to do?"

Without another word, Mama Z left the ruin. She didn't even have an umbrella. Connie, Mary Shelley, and I watched her go, getting soaked in seconds.

"This is awful. Nobody is going to help us," I moaned.

"It has to be you, Frank. Not Mama Z or your parents," Connie said. "Help us, like you promised." Connie clutched her flickering hands under her chin.

"I don't know if I can," I admitted.

Connie smiled softly at me. She seemed even more translucent now. I could see the veins in her face peeking through her freckles. Fear made my breath catch in my throat. I couldn't imagine being on Spectacle Key without Connie, and I'd do anything in the world to keep her with me. But time was not on our side. My only friend in the world was fading away before my eyes. "I believe in you," she said.

"Okay. I'll try," I said, sounding more confident than I felt. What I didn't say was that I had no idea where in the world to begin.

Chapter 20

NEVER MIND THE SWAMP APE!

In every city or town I'd ever lived in, I spent as much time as I could in the library, especially in the summers. Inside they always smelled the way most libraries do—like old paper with a touch of mold. Delicious! I'd make a stack of horror novels and sit at my favorite table and read until it was time to go. A librarian back in Alabama, Mrs. Andrews, would always let me check out the latest scary books first. One time she told me I was a "phobophile," which is a person who loves fear.

At the time, I'd liked that better than being called a "bookworm," which was what some of the guys at school had called me.

But as it turned out, I didn't love being afraid after all. Whenever Snuffles had acted up, I'd felt as if my stomach had liquefied and dropped straight into my ankles. Being afraid was a terrible thing, and the sound of Snuffles crying at the ruin, their voice completely shattered with fear, made me want to cry, too.

I watched Mama Z go out in the rainstorm. She was hunched over, probably thinking about her broken crystal ball. It had let us get in contact with Snuffles, but it hadn't fixed anything. Beside me, Connie flickered. Panicked, I riffled through the bag with the chemistry set in it. There had to be something in there that could help us. If science had brought Connie to Spectacle Key, maybe science could keep her there!

"That wasn't very helpful, was it?" Connie asked. "So much for crystal balls and such."

"You can say that again," I said, pushing aside microscope slides that clinked and snapped.

"So much for—" Connie started, but then realized what she was doing and stopped herself. "There has to be another way to get answers about this place, Frank."

"I'm trying," I said just as my hand fell on the magnifying glass Ms. McCartney had given me.

Maybe the clues that would help us solve the mystery of Spectacle Key weren't in séances, magic, or experiments. Maybe they were at the place where I always found answers.

"Hey, Connie, want to go to the library?"

Her mouth dropped open. "At a time like this? Trust me, Frank, you really don't need another scary book in your life."

"No," I said, and actually laughed. "We're going for research. Let's see what there is to learn about Spectacle Key. Maybe we can find out what really happened to this place."

Connie's whole face brightened. "Yes! That's very smart of you." Then she stepped out into the rain, completely unbothered.

A little sniff resounded in my ear. Now that I knew Snuffles was just a kid, I wasn't so afraid, even though I knew what they could do. "We're going to help, Snuffles. You can help, too, you know." I gestured at the downpour outside. I heard a sniff and the rain slowed to a trickle at once.

My breath caught in my throat. I'd suspected that Snuffles had something to do with the weird weather on Spectacle Key, but I wasn't sure until then. *Snuffles could drown us all in a tidal wave,* I thought, then brushed the idea away. It wasn't worth worrying about just yet.

Connie looked up at the suddenly blue sky in wonder. "Lucky us!" she said as I joined her.

"It's about time we had some luck," I said, and didn't mention Snuffles. Connie still kept her hands hidden, but every once in a while, I caught her peeking at them. She'd sigh a little, and I knew that her hands were still fading away.

The Tri-Key Library was a one-story concrete building. Outside, one wall was covered in a bright mural featuring dolphins underwater, nosing around colorful coral. A sign on the door said NO DOGS ALLOWED. I looked down at Mary Shelley, who was already looking at me with a sad face.

"Sorry, girl. Can you sit and wait? I'll give you a treat later." Mary Shelley sat at once in a shady spot near the front door. Connie and I walked inside, and I caught a whiff of that library aroma. The air-conditioning was blasting, too.

A young man in a guayabera shirt with a name tag that read "Manny Gomez" watched us from behind the lending desk. I went over. "Excuse me. Where can I find books about the Keys?" I asked.

Manny smiled big, like I was the first person to ask him for help in a long time.

"Come right this way," he said, leaping over the lending desk in one bound. He knocked over a stack of flyers, each with Ms. Emily Shiverton's face and the words *VOTE SHIVERTON FOR THE FLIPPY!* on it. Reluctantly, I helped Manny put the flyers back on the desk.

"That was a cool leap," I told him when we finished.

Manny beamed. "Former acrobat with the Florida Big Top Circus," he said, pointing at himself with his thumbs. Then he led us to a section of the library with low shelves. Conch shells were displayed on top of the bookcases, as were some special books on little stands. Manny gazed at the books for a while. I recognized that look on his face. Staring at rows of books sometimes felt like looking into a bakery window. I just wanted EVERYTHING.

"Are you new to the Keys?' Manny asked.

"Yep," I said. "I live in the lighthouse on Spectacle Key."

Manny bit his lip. "Oh," he said. "That's . . . rough."

"Yep," I repeated.

"Bad weather over there. Weird stuff," Manny said.

Beside me, Connie whispered, "He doesn't know the half of it."

"Yep," I said one more time.

"Well," Manny said, his tone lighter, "enjoy the history books. Lots to learn about the Keys! You should look up the Swamp Ape! Mysterious creature of the swaaaaaaamp," Manny added, making his voice go all low and spooky.

"Swamp Ape?" I asked, instantly hooked. "You mean there's a local monster and nobody's told me anything about it?"

Manny pointed at a pin I hadn't noticed underneath his name tag. It read *SWAMP APE DISCOVERY SQUAD*. "I'm a founding member of SADS." I wondered if there was a bylaw somewhere that stated that every club and organization in the Keys had to have a terrible acronym.

"Are there any comic books about it?" I asked, eager to learn more. But Connie stomped on my foot, bringing my focus back on the job at hand. "Never mind," I told Manny. "I—I'll look up the Swamp Ape later."

"Awesome, dude," Manny said, then returned to the lending desk.

"Let's not get distracted with any new monsters when you have two current monsters to deal with," Connie said angrily.

"You and Snuff aren't monsters," I said.

"Perhaps." Then she asked, "Snuff?"

I shrugged. "Why not. Maybe they'll like us more if we give them a nickname."

"Snuffles *is* a nickname," Connie reminded me, then started looking at the spines of all the books, her fingers trailing over them. Soon we had a stack of books to go through. Connie and I set them in piles around us on the floor in the kids' section, where paper-mache jellyfish hung from the ceiling and the carpet had a repeating sand dollar design on it. There were beanbags to sit on, and I had a view of Mary Shelley waiting patiently outside through the window.

Right away, we found a book titled *The Florida Keys: Weird and Funky,* and another called *Tiny but Mighty: Life in the Keys*. There was *Historical Keys: Uncovering the Secret Truths About Florida's Southernmost Islands,* and a whole bunch of others. I showed Connie how to read the index and the table of contents to quickly scan for mentions of Spectacle Key. Most of the time, there was nothing about the island. But every so often, Connie would shout, "Eureka!" and together we'd flip to the page that, supposedly, would lead to information about Spectacle Key.

"Missing," I said the first time we encountered the torn edge of a page ripped out of a book.

"This one, too," Connie added, showing me another book in which somebody had plucked out the Spectacle Key pages as if they were weeds in a garden.

We checked each and every book. Over and over, sections,

chapters, paragraphs, and photos of Spectacle Key had been destroyed.

"What could this mean?" Connie asked. All around us were books splayed open, the damage in them easy to see. It broke my heart. Books shouldn't be treated this way.

I sighed, closed all the books, and put the ruined ones in a pile for Manny to deal with. "It means that whatever happened on Spectacle Key was bad. So bad that someone is trying to erase it from history."

"Somebody sure has gone to a lot of trouble keeping Spectacle Key's past a secret. Are we ever going to figure this out?" Connie wondered. That's when I noticed that her hands were completely missing.

"Oh, Connie. I'm so sorry," I said softly, and pointed at her wrists.

She glanced down, then shook her head sadly. "I think I might be gone altogether soon."

Panic shot through me. Connie was my friend. My only friend in the whole world. "No! We're going to figure it out!"

Connie walked up to me and laid an invisible hand on my cheek. It was such a strange sensation, feeling her touch when I couldn't see it. "Promise you won't forget me, Frank Fernández," Connie whispered, her voice all wobbly.

"Never," I said. Funny thing, my voice had gone wobbly, too.

We took the stack of ruined books to Manny and explained what we'd noticed.

Manny took a deep breath and closed his eyes. "Monsters," he muttered, and he didn't mean the Swamp Ape. Manny looked all around, as if drinking in the library. "I love this place, you feel me? So much knowledge, so many stories. Your family keeps a lighthouse. I keep the library. Safe, I mean. When something like this happens—" Manny cradled a damaged book in his hands. "I feel bad, you know? I feel like, when a story gets forgotten, a part of the world goes with it." Tenderly, like he was handling living things, Manny gathered the ruined books into a stack. "Thanks for the heads-up, dude. Time to close up for the day anyhow."

Mary Shelley was waiting for me outside. Connie patted my dog's head with her invisible hands and Mary Shelley closed her eyes in pleasure at the feeling of being loved. I turned around to take another glance at the colorful library. I couldn't believe it had let me down. Even the library wasn't safe when it came to Spectacle Key. In the distance, the lighthouse was a smudge of white against the sky. Directly above it sat a dark cloud, like a sad hat.

With another defeated sigh, I led Connie and Mary Shelley back home.

Chapter 21

THE ZONING MEETING

Back on Spectacle Key, a white tent had been propped up in between the two "lenses" of the island while we'd been at the library. Cars were parked everywhere, right over the tall grasses, and people were crowding into the tent, where they sat on folding chairs.

"The zoning meeting!" I said, guilt making my stomach drop. "I completely forgot to tell Mom and Papi about the signs we saw!"

"That Ms. Shiverton and her HAUNT group are dastardly!" Connie said with a growl.

"I don't know what that means, but I agree with you," I said, and we took off running to warn my parents. We had to climb all the way to the top of the lighthouse to find them. Mom and Papi were working on the lighthouse lamp again.

They'd managed to patch the crack, but now the electricity was giving them trouble.

"Mom, Papi, you've gotta come quick," I said, panting.

Papi was wearing an old, holey T-shirt and paint-splattered jean shorts. "My working uniform," he called it. Mom was in overalls with a bandanna over her hair.

"Mister, now's not the time," Mom warned.

"But—" I started.

"Let us work, Junior," Papi mumbled. He held a thick pencil between his teeth, and also had one behind each ear. It was sweltering up there, and Papi had set up fans plugged into extension cords to keep the air moving and cool. Mom's cheeks were flushed as she positioned the lamp's mirrors, which would reflect the light for miles. Papi rummaged through his toolbox.

"You have to come," I continued. "They've set up a zoning meeting on the key. There are tons of people!"

The pencil dropped out of Papi's mouth. "¿Qué?" he asked.

"They're meeting about us and the lighthouse! Right now!" I shouted.

Mom was already pulling the bandanna off her hair. "Conveniently, we did not receive an invitation, did we?" she asked, and took off down the stairs.

"Wait for me!" Papi yelled, running after her.

Connie, Mary Shelley, and I followed. We could see the white tent and hear the murmur of the crowd that had gathered. As we drew nearer, someone began talking through a megaphone—it was Ms. Shiverton.

"People of the Florida Keys! We have fought off developers, oil companies, and unscrupulous hotel owners from our precious islands. Today, a new threat is upon us. The Fernández Home Conversion company has set up shop in our beloved lighthouse. Already they have endangered the island's blue crabs and coral passion vine. Who knows what they will chop up next?"

"WE DIDN'T CHOP UP ANY CRABS!" Mom roared as she ran into the tent. Her cheeks were blazing pink. Papi came up right behind her, nodding quickly.

"Ah, how kind of you to show up," Ms. Shiverton said to my parents, then added to the crowd, "See how little they care?" Everyone was holding a Flippy flyer with Ms. Shiverton's picture on it. Some people were using it as a fan to keep cool.

The murmurs grew louder. In the audience, I spotted Buzz wearing his Hawaiian shirt, Mr. McPhee in his bow tie, the twins, Minnie and Winnie, each holding identical clipboards, and Manny from the library and his fellow SADS members wearing their buttons. One of them had on a full Swamp Ape costume!

"Wow," I whispered.

"Don't get distracted," Connie warned.

"Right," I said, and made a mental note to research the Swamp Ape the next chance I got.

"What's the point of this meeting?" Mom demanded.

Ms. Shiverton pretended to shuffle through the papers in her clipboard. I could tell she already knew the answer. "We are voting on whether or not to recommend that the habitation status be removed from Spectacle Key. If we vote in favor of having Spectacle Key listed as a historic, uninhabitable island, then the motion goes to the mayor for final approval."

"¿Pero quien es el alcalde?" Papi asked the people around him.

Ms. Shiverton tsked. "They don't even know who the mayor is." All around us, people were shaking their heads.

Mom walked right up to Ms. Shiverton and snatched the megaphone out of her hands. "Now y'all listen up. My family has restored, and by restored I mean *saved,* countless important structures all over this country. Y'all are lucky, I mean *lucky,* that we have selected this island and that lighthouse, which is a hurricane away from coming apart at the darn seams. We'll get that lamp lit and make Spectacle Key a gosh darn *beacon* for this region, mark my words. And furthermore—"

Papi gently tugged the megaphone away from Mom. "And furthermore," he added. "We're good neighbors. Give us a chance to fix the lighthouse, get to know us. Just a chance, that's all we ask."

Buzz spoke up first. "The man knows how to handle a pair of garden shears."

Then Manny stood up and said, "Their son is a reader. Any kid who likes books is all right with me."

Connie leaned in to whisper in my ear. "They like your family, Frank. Maybe you'll get to stay after all!"

Sitting in the front row was Lucas. He turned around and gave me a thumbs-up again. Maybe he wasn't so bad.

But Ms. Shiverton wasn't having it. Taking the megaphone back, she shouted into it: "Don't be fooled! The Fernández family has lived in countless homes through the years. You think they're staying put? People like them are restless. They'll never make this their home. They'll never be our neighbors for good. Fixing things up and selling them to the highest bidder, that's what they do!"

My throat got very tight. Ms. Shiverton was saying out loud what I'd feared all along—that once my parents finished renovating the lighthouse, they'd get antsy, find a log cabin in Montana or a dilapidated ski lodge in Colorado, and we'd move again, leaving behind Connie, Snuffles, and Pop-Pop. It was a familiar fear, and it played out in my head like a movie. Mom and Papi would sit me down, their voices cheery as they described the next big move, and this time, I wouldn't even be able to tell them about the friend I'd made, because to them, she wasn't real. I blinked back tears as the meeting went on.

"How many cities have you lived in, anyway?" Buzz asked.

Mom and Papi looked at each other. "Eleven," Mom said.

"In how many years?" Mr. McPhee wondered.

"Eleven," Papi said.

People in the crowd gasped. Hearing the number out loud made me even sadder. It was true. I'd never lived in any place longer than a year. Would it be the same with Spectacle Key?

Conversations popped up all around us, with people shaking their heads. I overheard snippets of what they were saying:

"They'll make that lighthouse into a bed-and-breakfast, just you watch."

"Nobody ever lasts long on Spectacle Key. The place is spooky, if you ask me."

"What somebody *should* do is tear down that ruin on the other end of the island. It's dangerous."

I didn't hear anyone supporting us anymore. In fact, whenever anyone cut their eyes toward me, Mom, or Papi, it was with a look full of distrust. My heart sank. Mom and Papi held hands, but they kept their chins up. Ms. Shiverton started to pass around pieces of paper for a vote. She got them out to about half the crowd when the wind picked up, snatching the little sheets out of hands. The wind blew harder and harder.

SNIFF!

"Oh no. Snuffles!" Connie whispered frantically.

Mary Shelley walked around me in circles, her tail between her legs. Hats blew off people's heads, and soon they were shouting about the sand getting everywhere.

"The vote! The vote!" Ms. Shiverton said as a powerful blast of air sent her megaphone flying. The tent filled with air like a balloon and was soon lifted up, up, up. It flew far out over the ocean, carried away like a kite that had slipped away from its owner. After that, people scattered back to their cars. The smell of fruit was overwhelming, and some people even covered their noses with their shirts. Mom and Papi huddled over me. Ms. Shiverton grabbed Lucas's hand and they ran back to their vehicle, too.

At that point, the wind slowed and stopped.

"Oh, Snuffles," Connie said. "You're so sad and angry all the time," she whispered into the air.

When I looked at her, Connie was even more transparent than before. Every so often, she disappeared from view completely, like when the electricity cuts out during a storm for a second. Every time it happened, I held my breath, fearing that she'd stay gone. Moment by moment, Connie was slipping away.

"Let's go home," Papi said at last.

"Home?" Mom asked. "Are we sure it's still home?"

It felt like my family and I were slipping away from Spectacle Key, too.

In the distance, we could still see the tent soaring in the sky, like a lost zeppelin. I hoped it wouldn't land on a ship or hurt anybody out there. My parents talked about the meeting all the way back. Connie and I listened sadly. The closer we got to the lighthouse, the more defeated my parents seemed.

"I saw an ad for an abandoned courthouse in Ohio," I heard Papi say as we entered the lighthouse.

"No!" I shouted, making my parents jump. "I want to stay here. On this island, with Pop-Pop nearby and, and—" I couldn't quite finish the sentence. My folks thought Connie was imaginary. They'd just tell me she could come with me, which I wasn't even sure was true, and was something I didn't want to risk. What if Connie and Snuffles were bound to Spectacle Key?

"Mister," Mom sighed. "They just don't want us here."

"They will," I pressed on. "Let's fix the lamp. Then they'll see how beautiful we made the lighthouse. Don't give up, please," I said. I was crying by then, and snot was running horribly over my upper lip, all while Connie watched. If I wasn't so sad, I'd die of embarrassment.

Papi only shook his head. "Sometimes a lost cause is just that. Lost. I think we should start packing up."

Connie rested her head on my shoulder. "It's all right, Frank," she said. I realized I couldn't feel the weight of her head anymore.

It really isn't, I thought.

I looked down and noticed something. Connie's boots with the red laces were gone. Her legs stopped just above her ankles, so she looked like she was floating.

We were running out of time, and my parents were giving up at the worst moment.

Chapter 22

A TOUCH OF THE WIND

My parents had kept all the boxes we'd used to move. As soon as we got back to the lighthouse, they started pulling them out.

The whole time, I pleaded with them:

"The Fernández family never gives up!"

"We can't leave. We just got here."

"Don't let HAUNT win!"

"Think of Pop-Pop. He's not getting any younger, you know?"

But they didn't listen. Mom's shoulders sagged, and Papi looked like he'd just dropped an ice-cream cone with his favorite flavor in it. It must have been the curse, the same curse that made them fight all the time, and now had sapped them of their will to fight for our home.

"It's okay," Connie said from the foot of the stairs. She'd gone invisible below the knees, and the hem of her dress had started flickering. My green alligator T-shirt, which she still wore, seemed faded, too, as if it would soon disappear along with the rest of her. Mary Shelley sniffed the place where Connie's red-laced boots had been, whining quietly.

Papi handed me a stack of flattened boxes and some packing tape. "Better get to work, Frank."

"I don't want to. This is our home," I argued, but Papi only sighed and shook his head.

"Home is where you hang your hat, mister," Mom added, wrapping a vase in newspaper.

"I don't even own any hats!" I shouted, and turned and ran up the stairs. I could hear Connie running up after me on her invisible feet, and the clacking of Mary Shelley's nails on the wood. Even Snuffles was sniffing beside me.

That's the thing about Spectacle Key. Ever since I'd moved to the island, I hadn't been alone. I had Connie, for one. She was kind and understanding, plus she laughed at my jokes and didn't think it was strange that I loved books and monsters. Pop-Pop could come up on the weekends. Even Snuffles, who scared me out of my shoes most times, made me feel less lonely.

I must have been mumbling to myself when I entered my bedroom, because Connie asked, "What's that again?" When I looked at her, her right ear had gone missing. My voice caught in my throat.

"N-nothing," I said, and tried not to look at the hole where her ear had been. "I was just saying that when I'm a grown-up, I'm picking a place to live and never leaving it. Ever. I don't want to have to fill another stupid cardboard box in my whole adult life." I drop-kicked the stack of boxes, which fell with a thud and hurt my big toe, but not before knocking over the pile of books on my nightstand.

Connie and I went over to pick them up. Connie read the titles as she re-formed the book tower.

"Let's see. You've got *Frankenstein*."

"In abridged and comic book form," I added.

"A novel about Dracula's son?" she asked after looking at the back of the book.

"He's a painter in that one. And also a bloodsucking monster, naturally," I said.

"An encyclopedia on werewolves. Lovely." With a confused look on her face, Connie flipped through a novel about a yeti who goes to middle school in Paris.

"Ah, this one is cool! It's about a place called Zombie Beach!" I said, handing the book to Connie so that she could place it at the top of the stack.

"Last but not least," Connie said, lifting a book I hadn't had a chance to read yet.

"*Haunted Places in the Florida Keys!*" I exclaimed. It was my souvenir from the fish taco place I'd eaten at on the day we moved to Spectacle Key. "I forgot all about this one."

Connie snatched the book and started looking through the

index for the words *Spectacle Key*. "Aha!" she said. "Nobody got around to tearing anything out of *this* book, did they?" She turned to the pages and started reading, swatting me away as she nosed closer to the words. Soon, I could hear her breath catching, her fingers so tight on the book that the spine started to crackle in her grip.

"What is it?" I asked. Anxiety wrapped itself like a mattress spring around my stomach.

Connie looked up at me with very wide eyes. She said, "Just read it," with a croaky voice.

Gently, I took the book off her hands and looked at the page. It appeared to be a reprint of an old newspaper article, which read:

FOUNDLING LOST DURING HURRICANE

Work of the wind and tide

FORMER CARETAKERS UNSURE OF CHILD'S IDENTITY

Orphanage Forced to Close by Authorities

Spectacle Key, Florida—September 9, 1932—While the damage done by last week's hurricane was estimated by officials, the true scale of the loss was not apparent until this morning.

The Island Foundling Home, which houses and protects orphaned or abandoned babies and small children, took the brunt of the storm. Three caretakers, all sisters, evacuated the children before the hurricane struck land.

The sisters claim to have counted the children in their

care. However, now it is clear that they miscounted the innocent creatures, as one, a girl, has gone missing.

"She was a quiet child. So quiet, we often forgot about her," said Mary Trembly, the eldest. "But she did like to sing."

"What was the little boy's name again?" asked Clara Trembly, the youngest of the trio.

"It was a girl, remember?" clarified Mary.

"Alice something or other, I think," affirmed middle sister Jane Trembly.

Clara added, "Her surname had a touch of the wind in it, isn't that so?"

"Yes, quite apt," Jane retorted.

All three have expressed great sadness at the loss of this woebegone, forgotten child.

In response, authorities have closed the Island Foundling Home, citing neglect and improper care. The remaining children will be moved to a home in Miami.

As for the house itself on Spectacle Key, it took a pounding from the sea, and was declared unfit for habitation by the local government.

"Frank," Connie whispered, out of breath and clutching her face. "Could I be the 'woebegone, forgotten child'?"

"You might be," I said, and felt a wave a sadness. Someone as good and fun as Connie didn't deserve to be woebegone, whatever that meant. Nobody did, really.

Snuffles snorted loudly.

Connie reread the article. "Alice," she breathed out. "My name is Alice."

Now that she'd said so, it felt right. Connie was an Alice, I was certain. And just like Alice in Wonderland, she'd fallen through a rabbit hole and disappeared from the world.

"Alice," I said out loud, testing the name out. Her boots appeared again. "Alice!" I shouted. Suddenly, her right ear came back into view, as did her feet! "Alice! Alice! Alice!" I said, and now her hands started glimmering, faintly at first and then returning once more. Alice flexed her fingers and then tickled me all over.

"Stop!" I yelled laughing so hard tears leaked from the corners of my eyes.

"Say uncle!" Alice demanded with a giggle.

"Huh?" I gasped.

Alice stepped back, catching her breath. "It's a game we played when I was, um, around the first time. You're supposed to say 'Uncle!' and then I stop tickling you."

"Oh. Sorry. I'll say it next time," I told her, and wondered what it must have been like for Alice growing up so long ago, playing weird games, having no idea what a television was, or a video game.

"I *do* feel like an Alice!" she said all in a rush, patting herself all over as if she'd only just now realized she was in one piece again.

"And if we know your name . . . ," I began.

"We can speak the name of the lost child!" Alice cheered, standing on her now-solid feet. "And maybe that locked door in the ruin will open and give us more clues!" She ran out, half skipping down the stairs.

I thought of Snuffles. "Well, one of the lost children, at least. Maybe it's enough."

"Wait up!" I shouted behind her. Mary Shelley brought up the rear, Bernard in her jaws, as the three of us tore out of the lighthouse, whizzing past my parents, who were so busy packing up everything we owned that they didn't notice me leaving.

I was full of hope. If we could speak the name of the lost child, then maybe the curse on Spectacle Key would be lifted for good. My parents would be back to their old selves. The weird weather would stop. There would be no more crab invasions, or out-of-control plants. Maybe even the members of HAUNT would leave us alone. Could the curse on Spectacle Key be what made Ms. Shiverton so mean and spiteful? Anything was possible!

Alice, it turned out, was a very fast runner. Every so often, she'd laugh and say her own name, "ALICE!" Until suddenly, as we nearly reached the ruin, she stopped cold.

"Oh," she said quietly, then sat down among the tall grasses in an ungraceful plop. A pair of orange butterflies flew up around her and flitted away.

"What's wrong?" I asked. Mary Shelley headbutted Alice tenderly.

"The article, Frank. It says that Alice, that's me, was left behind during a storm. That's how I must have died. And I lived in a home for foundlings. Do you know what a foundling is?"

I shook my head. I hadn't thought about what else the article had revealed because I'd been so happy to learn Alice's real name. She was right. This was awful news.

"It means orphan. It means that my momma, the one I remembered, had to leave me for some reason. Or maybe she . . . maybe she—" Alice couldn't speak any further. She drew her knees up and rested her forehead on them, crying softly. I wondered how Alice had felt back when she was alive, all alone in the Island Foundling Home without her momma. Had anybody comforted her? Had anybody been a friend?

This time, I knew what to do. I sat down beside her and held her hand until she was done crying. I'd stay there all day if I had to. Ghost or not, Alice needed me. I didn't say anything, because there wasn't anything I could tell her that she hadn't already thought of. Snuffles was also there, and I could have sworn I heard them crying, too, like a faraway sound being carried by the wind. Mary Shelley put Bernard on Alice's lap and leaned against her, licking her cheeks every so often.

"You aren't alone anymore, Alice," I said after a while.

"Thank you, Frank," she said, then dried her eyes with my alligator T-shirt. She stood up and dusted off her dress.

"Let's go tell my name to a pantry door and be rid of this curse once and for all."

Alice was very brave. It made me feel brave, too.

"For what it's worth, I'll bet your momma loved you a lot," I consoled her.

"I know she did, Frank. I can feel it right here," she said, and patted her chest.

After that, we didn't run. Slowly and silently, we made our way back to the abandoned building. It wasn't just a ruin anymore. It was the place where something unspeakable had happened, where Alice had lost her life because of three irresponsible caretakers. Stepping through the arch and onto the tiled floor felt somber now, like walking into a church during a funeral. The letters *IFH* met us everywhere. *Island Foundling Home,* I reminded myself, and thought of the crib and bed upstairs, the baby bottle, the lost boot. How many children had lived here? Had Alice stood with them around the mosaic and sung the national anthem each morning, like she'd seen in her memory? Had Georgia Finkel jumped rope in the yard while picking her nose here? What had Alice's life been like before the storm?

Our footfall on the sand-covered ground was quiet. Even Mary Shelley trod gently. In the kitchen, we entered the pantry.

Breathing deeply, I tried the doorknob again, just in case.

Snuffles released three loud snorts, hurrying us along.

"Let's do this," I said.

"Ready?" Alice asked.

I nodded in agreement. Then, using the loudest voice I had, I yelled, "The lost child is named Alice!" My voice echoed all over the building. Snuffles sniffed like crazy, making Mary Shelley snap at the air.

But the door did not open.

"Come on!" I shouted in anger, kicking the door. Alice was frustrated, too, and she sent an old aluminum can skittering across the kitchen.

Now what do we do? I wondered.

"Maybe I need to speak my last name as well," Alice said, and I groaned. As long as somebody was tampering with the information at the library, we might never find out Alice's full name, if it was ever listed anywhere in the first place.

Alice and I paced the kitchen, thinking hard. "Snuffles, you might have to be more specific there, buddy," I said to the air. "Will we need to know her middle name, too? And her social security number?"

SNIFF!

A cabinet fell off the wall in the kitchen with a mighty crash.

"Don't tease Snuffles, remember?" Alice said, panic in her voice.

Mary Shelley had been chewing on Bernard's hat for a while. Not much was left of the little sailor cap, and Bernard, who was dingy to begin with, now looked absolutely revolting. Suddenly Bernard tumbled along the floor, led by an invisible hand.

SNIFF!

This time, a kitchen drawer shot open, and a rusty knife floated out of it before clattering to the floor.

"Sorry! Won't make fun, I promise!" I shouted. My knees knocked together in fear. Snuffles was angry and impatient.

"If that doll's head starts spinning again, I'm going to faint," Alice said weakly.

Snuffles seemed to be dragging Bernard to the pantry. A jangling sound caught my attention as the little key around Bernard's neck scraped the tile floor.

Wait, the key! I thought. *But it couldn't be that simple, could it?*

I dashed into the pantry and grabbed Bernard, who was sticky with drool. Alice soon joined me. With a quick tug, I tore the skeleton key off Bernard's neck.

"You think it will work?" I asked Alice.

"We have to try," she responded.

SNIFF, went Snuffles.

"Snuffles agrees," I said, hoping I was right.

The key turned easily in the lock. I took hold of the glass doorknob, gave it a twist, and . . .

Whoosh!

The door opened, releasing a gust of stale air.

I took a giant whiff, and you know what it smelled like?

Like mold. Like paper, breaking down over time.

It was a heavenly, familiar smell.

Beside me, Alice murmured in wonder at the sight of what had been hidden behind the door. "Oh, Frank. It's a—"

"A library!" I rejoiced.

Chapter 23

MEMORIES

It wasn't a large library. Not much bigger than my bedroom, really. But there were bookcases all around, two dusty leather chairs in one corner, and an actual library ladder to reach the top shelves! Mary Shelley jumped onto one of the chairs, a cloud of dust forming around her. She'd taken Bernard back, and now held the doll tightly under her massive paws. All this time, Snuffles hadn't been trying to scare us by moving Bernard—they'd been showing us the key we needed!

Running in excitement to the nearest shelf, I touched a book, which was spongy from the damp. "Everything's ruined," I sighed in disappointment.

Alice spun slowly in the center of the room. "I remember sitting just here," she said, pointing at the floor. "While somebody, a grown-up, sat there, reading a story." She indicated one of the chairs. I wondered what the kids who lived at the IFH had read, and whether stories helped them forget their troubles.

SNIFF, went Snuffles.

"Sounds like Snuff's glad we found this place," I commented, feeling a little relieved. Even though Snuffles was terrifying at times, it felt like I was beginning to understand them a bit. Maybe it was the same way I could figure out how Mary Shelley was feeling through barks and growls.

"I agree. What did you want us to find, Snuffles?" Alice asked.

At once, Snuffles began to sniffle all over the library, the sound settling finally over a large wooden box on one of the lower shelves.

"Check this out," I said, pulling the box onto the floor. Alice and I sat before it. The whole time Snuffles made lots of noise. "Okay, okay, hold your horses."

"Or hold your noses, in Snuffles's case," Alice added.

SNIFF, went Snuffles, as if telling us to stop wasting time.

I lifted the lid on the box. Inside were yellow files. The first had the name of a girl on the outside—Molly Shirley—written in fading blue ink. I opened it and found a picture, warped from the moisture in the room, of a girl posing for a portrait while sitting on a wooden chair. The other papers in her file included her birth certificate, her health records, and more photographs.

"Do you remember her?" I asked Alice, who shook her head sadly.

"Frank, maybe there's a file here about me," she said. We looked through them all, even finding a file on Georgia the Nose Picker. Snuffles was quiet the whole time. Finally, only the last file remained in the box.

"This has to be it," I said. Trembling, I drew the final folder out and turned it over. There, written in blue ink, was a name: *Alice Gale.*

Alice gasped beside me, reaching out to touch her name with her fingertips. "Open it," she whispered.

So I did. Inside, looking back at us, was a torn picture of Alice, smiling and holding the hand of a dark-haired woman. They were both wearing straw hats tied under their chins with a broad ribbon, and both wore the same happy smile. A portion of the photograph was missing to Alice's left, but the people in the picture remained.

"Momma!" Alice gushed, lifting the picture and crushing it against her lips in a kiss. "Oh, Momma!" She cried and cried, looking through the papers that told her all about herself—how Alice had been born in a small Florida town called Immokalee in December of 1921, and how her mother and father had been tomato farmers. Her father died when Alice was a baby, and by the time she was ten years old, her mother could no longer afford to keep her safe and sound, so Alice was given up to the Island Foundling Home. It had been a hard life for Alice and her parents, but in the picture

I could tell how much her mother had wanted her, and I imagined it must have been terrible to say goodbye.

Alice read everything in silence. Finally, turning over the last piece of paper, Alice looked up at me with shining eyes. "I remember almost everything," she said, exhaling loudly.

"Almost?" I asked.

Alice nodded. "Some of the memories are blurry. Parts are missing. But even so. I remember *Momma*."

"Is that a good thing?" I wondered. Maybe she was better off not remembering the sad story of her life. Maybe it was better if all Alice knew was Spectacle Key, Mary Shelley, and me. As soon as I asked it, I realized it had been a selfish question. I'd hate not knowing about myself.

Alice nodded. "It's a wonderful thing. But it's not easy realizing that everyone I ever knew is long dead. Or that those terrible caretakers at the IFH forgot I existed and left me alone here during a hurricane." Alice's nose was running, and she was sniffing right along with Snuffles. The room must have been very dusty because my eyes were stinging and my nose was running, too, though I'm not sure Alice believed me when I muttered, "Dust."

Then, as if she'd just realized something, Alice clutched my hand and turned to face me. "Frank! You know my story now. I'm no longer the lost child of Spectacle Key, which means—"

"That the curse on Spectacle Key is now lifted!" I said. I punched the air above my head and went "Woo-hoo!" a few times. Alice twirled around me. It was finally going to be okay.

SNIFF!

Snuffles, I realized, the joy I'd been feeling evaporating at once. We'd been focusing so much on Alice that I hadn't stopped to wonder what had happened to Snuffles, who must have suffered along with Alice.

"Were you left behind during the storm?" I asked Snuffles. A cool breeze swept the back of my neck, like an icy finger. I clamped my hand on the skin there and stifled a terrified shout.

Alice sucked her teeth as if she'd just bitten into something freezing cold. She took a deep breath before asking, "I wasn't the only child left to bear a terrible fate during the hurricane, was I?"

"It's worse than that," I said. "The caretakers didn't even *remember* that they *forgot* Snuffles."

Papers fluttered lightly around us and a breeze tickled our hair. It was sweet-smelling, like being breathed on by somebody who'd just had a lollipop.

The box of files! I thought. Alice must have had the same idea, because we rummaged through them again, naming all the children we could find.

"Georgia Finkel!"

"Molly Shirley!"

"Rogelio Acosta, is that you, Snuffles?"

"Lester Goranovsky, maybe?"

On and on we went, reading the names, and each time,

Snuffles only sniffed sadly. When we got to the bottom of the box, Snuffles started to wail, at first right into our ears so that we screamed and slapped our hands over them, and then off they went, crying into the distance, far, far away.

"They really forgot all about them," I said.

Alice nodded sadly. "Snuffles is the completely lost child of Spectacle Key." She sat down among the files on the floor of the library. Drops of sweat gathered at her temples. I wasn't sure I'd ever seen Alice sweat, though it had been super hot the whole time I'd been on Spectacle Key. She was getting more real and solid by the minute. In fact, it seemed that the more I learned about Alice, the less like a ghost she seemed. Maybe Alice and Mama Z were right all along. Maybe Alice had never been a ghost.

Alice began to gather some of the files into her lap. "We should take these to Manny at the library. The Spectacle Key books might be destroyed, but the fate of the Island Foundling Home is a history worth remembering, don't you think?"

"Alice!" I shouted, then gave her a huge hug. "I figured it out! Manny said that when a story gets forgotten, a part of the world goes with it, remember?"

Alice nodded.

"So you aren't a ghost, Alice Gale. You're a . . . a . . . a memory! And the longer you were forgotten, the further you faded away!"

Alice got to her feet, clutching files to her chest. "But then you and your family moved to Spectacle Key, and you came to the IFH building and somehow brought me back!"

The building groaned around us, as if it were living and remembering. "And this place," I whispered. "What happened here has been covered up for so long that the whole island got cursed."

Alice shivered all over, despite the sweat. "That sounds about right."

Suddenly the heavy, damp books all around us slipped off their shelves. A dictionary thumped me on the head, while a pop-up book on castles fell wetly all over Alice. "Snuffles, stop!" I yelled, but that only made things worse, and the books began to fall more forcefully.

"We still don't know Snuffles's name," Alice said. A dictionary fell at her feet, and she yelped, jumping backward. "Momma always said that when someone is hurt they often make bad choices, and Snuffles has been hurt terribly."

The tiles underneath our feet began to buckle and snap; shards of porcelain tile went zipping in the air and lodged themselves into the walls. "Snuffles!" I shouted. "We figured out Alice's story. We'll figure yours out, too!"

But I didn't think Snuffles was listening to us anymore. We could hear them crying as they sent more and more items flying. Alice grabbed the box of files and we ran out of the secret room. Mary Shelley panted beside me. Behind us, Snuffles destroyed the library, and I turned around to see one of the chairs floating in the air, then smashing to the floor and breaking in pieces.

"Snuffles, no," I whispered, the obliterated library breaking my heart.

We ran until we were clear of the ruin. There was nothing left to learn in that place. We'd discovered all we could about Alice, and as far as we could tell, the caretakers hadn't kept a single record about Snuffles.

"This is impossible," I said at last, leaning over and gripping my knees. "We'll never figure out Snuffles's real name, or who they were. We'll never be able to remember them. We need to know the whole story of Spectacle Key if we're going to lift the curse."

"And bring the memory of Snuffles back," Alice added.

"Plus, it's the only way I'm going to get to stay here." We were both quiet after that. I didn't want to think of moving again, or of leaving Alice and Pop-Pop behind. It made my throat feel all tight. "Dust," I said, and wiped my eyes, but Alice was staring at the IFH building.

"What's the worst Snuffles can do?" she asked. In the distance, a boom sounded from deep within the ruin. A giant flamboyán tree beside what was left of the IFH creaked and shook, started to lean, and finally crashed into the roof, its giant roots exposed in the air like great brown tentacles.

Alice gritted her teeth. "Well, that answers that."

Alice, Mary Shelley, and I observed the destruction for a few minutes. The walls trembled and it was as if we could feel Snuffles's anger in the vibrations beneath our feet.

Alice had removed her mother's picture from her file and tucked it into her apron pocket. "I think I know a bit about how Snuffles feels. But me? I feel fluttery. Happy, warm flutters. I think it's peace that I feel inside," she said after a while. "Like I'm myself again. Connie was a good name, but Alice is better. I was very good at jump rope. Now I remember. Even better than Georgia Finkel. And I won the spelling bee at IFH the year I was there. And I know how to grow a tomato so that it's the juiciest thing you ever ate. I didn't remember myself until now, and it feels, it feels—" She stopped to think for a bit. "Oh, Frank, it feels like everything is beautiful and right with me again."

In the distance, a part of IFH's roof crumbled like a stale cookie. The crash was so loud that Alice and I covered our ears. Dust formed like a cloud over the IFH before settling down again. I broke out into an instant sweat, and I noticed that Alice was biting the corner of her lip and trying not to cry.

She pulled herself together pretty quickly. "We need to give that peace back to Snuffles. That's why I returned to Spectacle Key. I just know it."

I looked at Alice with new eyes. She was determined, her mouth set in a firm line. Her eyes sparkled, and even her freckles looked brighter against her skin. Moment by moment, she looked less like a ghost and more like a regular girl. She made me feel courageous.

"You're right. We can do this," I said.

The noises from the ruin settled down at last. I wondered what Snuffles was feeling. They were probably furious that we'd figured out Alice's story while their's remained a mystery. Then again, Snuffles had led us to the library. Snuffles was helpful, in their own way. But Snuff's pain was like having a cut that kept bleeding, no matter how many bandages you put on it.

Still, there was no doubt that Snuffles was scary. If they could topple a building like the IFH, I shuddered to think of what could happen to the lighthouse. And what if everyone I loved was in it while Snuffles threw another tantrum? Would Snuffles destroy Spectacle Key in the end? What if I became a lost child, too? Pop-Pop wouldn't be around forever, and he was all the family we had left. Who would remember me then?

Chapter 24

MS. SHIVERTON'S SECRET

Snuffles followed us all the way back to the lighthouse, ripping through bushes and kicking up plumes of sand. When Snuffles yanked Alice's braids, she shouted, "You're being especially naughty. Stop it at once!" and Snuffles calmed down at last.

"That was very brave," I whispered, impressed. My legs felt like spaghetti.

Alice shook her head the tiniest bit and adjusted her braids. "I'm scared, too, Frank."

That made me feel a little better. "Papi always says that bravery is the ability to face scary things, even though you're still scared," I told her.

"That's us, then. At least, I hope we can be that," Alice said.

"I hope so, too."

Once at the lighthouse, we found nearly everything already in boxes. I climbed over them to get to the kitchen, with Alice and Mary Shelley trailing behind me.

"I'm going to try to talk my parents out of moving off the island," I told Alice. "Snuffles still needs us." I didn't want to leave Snuff and Alice alone on Spectacle Key. They'd already been abandoned once, after all. "Mom, Papi," I called, jumping over a box labeled *PAPI'S TOOLS—NO TOCAR!* When I reached the kitchen, to my astonishment I saw my parents sitting at the table with Ms. Shiverton.

"Hello, young man," she said.

"Uh, hello," I responded. My mom was sitting up very straight and her hands were on her lap. I could see them gripping her knees through the glass tabletop. Papi was resting his chin on one hand. Spread out on the table was a lot of paperwork.

Ms. Shiverton smiled tightly at me. She wore a button with her face on it that read, *A FLIPPY FOR EMILY!* "I'm sorry you won't get to be classmates with my Lucas in the fall. He's a top student, and an excellent example to others."

"I won't?" I asked. It's not like I was desperate to be Lucas's pal after everything that had happened, but I had been looking forward to attending middle school in the Keys.

"Sorry, mister," Mom said.

"It's for the best," Papi added.

I looked at the paperwork Ms. Shiverton and my parents

were in the midst of signing. I saw a seller's and buyer's contract, and the address for the lighthouse listed on every page.

"You're selling the lighthouse? To HER?" I demanded.

"¡Oye!" Papi shouted.

"Manners, mister!" Mami bellowed.

I turned around and saw Alice hiding behind boxes in the living room, chewing on her fingernails. Mary Shelley waited with her. I shook my head in her direction, and Alice covered her face with her hands.

Ms. Shiverton smiled haughtily. "I will become caretaker of the lighthouse at last. It makes sense, as my family has lived in the Keys for many generations. You can be assured that I'll be a responsible owner." Something in her voice seemed to suggest that we had been anything but responsible. Mom's cheeks flushed pink and Papi's nostrils flared.

"Okay, but will you love it? Like we do? Even if this place is a total pain?" I asked.

Ms. Shiverton observed me for a moment, then said, "Love has nothing to do with it."

"What about the ruin on the other side of the key?" I demanded.

"Demolishing it the first chance I get," she said.

Poor Snuffles, I thought. How would everyone remember what had happened there once it was gone for good?

The doorbell rang. I remembered the ding-dong-ditcher when we'd first moved in. It must have been Snuffles then. *Riiiing* went the doorbell again, more insistently this time.

What if Snuffles was back? Were we in danger?

Papi rose to open the door, and I followed him. Mary Shelley was barking up a storm, up on her hind legs and pawing at the locks.

"How can I help you?" Papi asked as he pushed the door open.

There stood Mama Z in a business suit, her red hair pulled back in a bun and a leather briefcase in her hand.

"Allow me to introduce myself. My name is Zoraya Zamora, mayor of Spectacle Key."

"What?" I exclaimed.

Alice was beside me at once. "Why didn't you tell us, Mama Z?" she asked, but Mama Z didn't answer. Instead, she looked at me and Alice and gave us a wink.

"Might I find Emily Shiverton here?" Mama Z asked, patting her briefcase.

Papi looked resigned and a little nervous. "Are we in trouble? Because we're selling. It's what you people wanted, after all."

Mama Z huffed and sucked her teeth. "Nonsense," she said, and before Papi could utter another word, she pushed past us and headed to the kitchen.

Mom was busy signing page after page. "All we need are my husband's signatures and the deal is done," she was saying glumly while Ms. Shiverton looked on with a smile.

"Good afternoon," boomed Mama Z, and both Mom and Ms. Shiverton jumped out of their chairs.

"Mayor Zamora!" Ms. Shiverton said, smiling so widely I thought her face would get stuck that way. "What are you doing here?"

Mama Z surveyed the room slowly. She glanced at the sale papers and her nostrils flared. Then she fixed her gaze onto Ms. Shiverton's, as if magnets had brought them together. "I happened to go by the library this morning for the weekly Read It and Weep Book Club meeting, when I had a little chat with Manny the librarian. He mentioned this." Mama Z pulled one of the damaged books Alice and I had found out of her bag.

Ms. Shiverton's eyes widened.

"Emily," Mama Z began, "how long have you been president of HAUNT?"

Proud as a peacock, Ms. Shiverton pretended to tally up the years. "Since its founding, actually," she said at last.

When nobody was looking, Mom rolled her eyes at me. Papi had joined us in the kitchen, and he huffed in frustration.

"And to be clear, it's a historical society, yes?" Mama Z asked.

"Of course," Ms. Shiverton said.

Pulling out a chair for herself, Mama Z sat and began riffling through her briefcase. Her fingertips danced over the edges of folders until, finally, she licked her thumb and pulled out a single sheet of paper, which she laid on the table and pushed toward Ms. Shiverton.

"What's this?" she asked.

Mama Z flattened her palm on the page. "Five years' worth of overdue library fees. Every book you've checked out and not returned has been on the history of Spectacle Key. I asked Manny to let me know who had shown such a keen interest in this key, and the answer was you, Emily. Furthermore, Manny has informed me that there has been extensive damage to historical material in the library, and that after reviewing security tapes, you were caught tearing pages out of the books."

Ms. Shiverton sat very silently and very still.

Mom and Papi looked from Mama Z to Ms. Shiverton, back and forth like they were watching a tennis match.

"Why?" I asked. "Why would you destroy books? What did they ever do to you?"

"Ah, Frank," Mama Z said. "The books didn't do anything to her. She was trying to cover up a nasty history."

"This must be about IFH," Alice said.

Ms. Shiverton stuck her nose up in the air. "I have no idea what you're talking about."

Mama Z narrowed her eyes, took a deep breath, and dug into her briefcase for another piece of paper. "Aha!" she said, finding the form she was looking for. The top of the page read *PETITION FOR A CHANGE OF NAME*. "You weren't always Emily Shiverton, were you, Emily *Trembly*?"

Suddenly, Ms. Shiverton grew very pale. "How dare you look through my personal records?"

"Public records," Mama Z clarified. It was so strange to

see her in a suit, without her long skirts, beaded necklaces, and crystal ball. I wondered if she'd used her crystal ball to figure out Ms. Shiverton, or if she'd used good old-fashioned research.

"I won't stand for these—these LIES!" Ms. Shiverton screeched. Mary Shelley covered her head with her paws.

Searching through her briefcase again, Mama Z found what she wanted and began to read. "The Trembly sisters, caretakers of the Island Foundling Home, are your ancestors, isn't that so?"

Ms. Shiverton pursed her lips. Mama Z went on.

"You've been very busy covering up their shameful negligence, haven't you?"

"Do you realize that I'm a finalist for the Flippy!" Ms. Shiverton cried, tears in her eyes.

"Yes, everyone knows. You keep reminding us," Mom said.

"If word got out that my great-grandmother and her sisters let a child die in a hurricane, it would ruin *everything* for me!" Ms. Shiverton said.

"How horrible for you," Papi added in a tone that seemed to suggest he didn't mean a single syllable of it.

"Not just one child. TWO," I said, and Ms. Shiverton wailed even more loudly. "You shouldn't be president of a historical society when you're trying to cover up history, even if it is an ugly one."

"It isn't MY fault!" Ms. Shiverton cried. "I didn't have anything to do with what happened to that orphanage!"

"Indeed you didn't," Mama Z said. "This is true. But one must face their history and, whenever possible, work to right wrongs. Besides, you can't expect to win a Flippy when you've been trying to drive away this very nice family for fear that they might discover your secret. Also, as I've mentioned, you're five years behind on library dues. Please return the historical Spectacle Key books at once."

Ms. Shiverton took a deep breath, muttered something about lawyers, and left the lighthouse.

The pieces were coming together in my mind. Ms. Shiverton, Alice, Snuffles, the IFH, and my family coming back here. *Read between the lines,* I thought. I turned to Alice, whispering hurriedly, "Now I know why you and Snuffles showed up when my family moved here! Ms. Shiverton was going to destroy any chance of either of you being remembered."

Alice's eyes were shiny with tears. "You and your family saved us, Frank."

SNIFF, went Snuffles. Alice and I went very still at the noise, even though, to me, it sounded more sad than angry.

"Not yet," I said. "We still have work to do."

Mom and Papi sat there in stunned silence. "I don't think I want to sign these sales contracts anymore," Papi said, and Mom agreed.

Alice crushed me in a hug. "You're staying, Frank! Staying!"

Mama Z gathered her papers back into her briefcase

and spoke to my parents. "If you're going to remain, then you'll need to be keepers not only of a lighthouse, but of its history and the history of this island, as well as those who once called it home. The Emily Shivertons of the world will always try to cover up the darkness of the past, when what it needs, most of all, is a light to shine upon it. It's the only way we learn as humans." Mama Z looked directly at Alice, giving her another wink.

Could she *see* Alice now? Alice took my hand and squeezed it hard. I could feel her pulse pounding in her fingertips. Mine matched hers, beat for beat.

"We're up to the task, Mayor," Papi said.

"Indeed," Mom added, then tore up the sales contract. "But I'm not sure I understand what happened here."

Mama Z glanced over at me. "I think Frank can explain it better than I can."

I gave Mama Z a thumbs-up.

"Are we home, then? For good?" I asked.

"Please say yes," whispered Alice.

"For good," Mom and Papi said at the same time.

Alice and I chased after Mama Z, who was already headed for the front door. Alice tugged on Mama Z's long skirt, and the mayor turned around and squinted at Alice. "I see you, Connie," she whispered. "You're shimmery, a faint image. But you're there. A person has to be perceptive, you understand, and I am very perceptive." She smiled. "I like your boots, though I do think that alligator T-shirt clashes a bit."

"It's Alice, actually. Alice Gale," she said, and Mama Z's eyes widened.

"Curious how some things are kept secret!" Mama Z said. "But when they are revealed, the truth comes tumbling out at once!"

"It's nice to meet you again," Alice replied.

"It's nice to meet you, mi niña. Adios to you both. A mayor's work is never done!" Mama Z said, then flounced out the door.

"Frank!" Mom and Papi called at the same time. "Help us unpack!"

I whooped with joy! "Best chore ever!" I answered.

Chapter 25

HURRICANE

That afternoon, I told Mom and Papi everything.

They really didn't like that I'd snuck off the island to go to Mama Z's, and that I hadn't mentioned the time I'd gone to the library. That was a big rule for them—"Always tell us where you're going"—and I'd broken it.

But they got so interested in my story that they seemed to forget all about grounding me. When I started to describe who Connie-turned-Alice had been in life, Mom gasped.

"Is tha-that *her*?" Mom asked, pointing right where Alice was standing.

"I think I see her, too!" Papi said. "It wasn't heatstroke after all, was it?"

Mom and Papi had to squint to see Alice, and when she spoke to them ("How do you do, Mrs. and Mrs. Fernández?")

they heard it as a very faraway whisper. Still, it was something.

"She's a memory," I explained. "Almost completely forgotten except for the article in this book." I showed them *Haunted Places in the Florida Keys* and Alice's file from the IFH.

"I came back to make sure I'd be remembered," Alice said. Mom and Papi read over her file, and every once in a while, one of them would lift their eyes and give Alice a sad look. I knew they were imagining all that Alice had been through, wishing they could make it better.

"Earlier, you mentioned that *two* children had been lost," Mom put in.

I cleared my throat. Snuffles would be harder to explain. Would my parents want to sell the lighthouse after all once they learned the chaos Snuffles had caused, and what they could do?

"Tell them," Alice urged.

"Well, there's Snuffles," I began.

"Snuffles?" my parents asked at the same time.

"Mm-hmm. Snuff was abandoned at the IFH, too. But there are no records of them. We don't know their real name or anything," I explained.

"Snuffles has been completely forgotten," Alice added.

SNIFF!

My parents startled at the sound. *Be nice, Snuffles,* I thought, worried that Snuff might lose their temper again.

"That's Snuffles," I said. "They snuffle a lot. Hence, the nickname."

Mom held Papi's hand and squeezed. "Hello, Snuffles," she whispered.

Snuffles didn't answer.

"Maybe we can try a different library," Papi said to the air around him. "Find out your name, buddy."

Alice clapped. "Your parents are so helpful! Like you, Frank." Then she leaned over and kissed my cheek. Thankfully, Mom and Papi missed it as they looked over the IFH papers some more.

When Mom looked up, she asked, "You okay, mister? You look a little flushed." She patted my face, and beside me, Alice giggled.

Suddenly, the doorbell rang for a long time. I thought it was Snuffles again, playing tricks.

"I'll get it," I rushed to say. My parents weren't quite ready for one of Snuffles's outbursts. They had enough to get used to, and the last thing I needed was for them to change their minds about staying in Spectacle Key. Taking a deep breath, I turned the knob and . . .

There, silhouetted in the dark, was a tall figure holding something enormous.

"Is that—" I started to ask when I was interrupted by a loud voice.

"I'm moving in with y'all!" shouted Pop-Pop. He was holding a box of his stuff!

"What?" I exclaimed.

Mom greeted him, saying, "Daddy! You really want to move in with us?"

Pop-Pop beamed and pulled her into a hug.

"Welcome home, then," Papi said.

Alice cheered, and Pop-Pop dropped the box he'd been holding right on his toes. "What in glimmering tarnation is that?" he asked, pointing at Alice with one hand and rubbing one of his feet with the other.

It would take a while to explain it all again, but I was getting good at telling the story of Spectacle Key. Papi thought it was a tale best told over Cuban coffee, even if it was late at night. So he fired up the cafetera and the adults drank and talked, showing Pop-Pop the IFH files and telling him all about the curse on Spectacle Key. As a scientist through and through, I figured he would have a hard time believing everything that had happened, and part of me was afraid he'd load his car up again and return to Miami. But as usual, Pop-Pop surprised me.

"So, technically, the place is still cursed?" Pop-Pop asked when we were done.

"It will be until we figure out Snuffles's real name, I think," I said.

SNIFF, went Snuffles.

"Ah," Pop-Pop said. "This is a real conundrum. I love conundrums." He rubbed his big palms together and they made a sound like a breeze through the tall grass. "We'll figure it out, sonny boy."

"I love your family," Alice whispered.

"Me too," I told her.

Pop-Pop settled into his chair once he finished his coffee. He pulled a pen and small notepad out of his back pocket. At the top of the page he wrote *Alice!* and underlined it twice. "Time to get sleuthing," he announced.

"Sleuthing?" I asked.

Pop-Pop gave me a crooked smile. "Means we're gonna figure this here problem out. Good scientists are like detectives, sonny boy. Now, young lady," he began, turning toward Alice, "what do you remember about your life on Spectacle Key?"

Yes, I thought. Pop-Pop was going into full science mode and I had a first-row seat!

Alice cleared her throat. "I don't remember most things about my life here, sir. There are gaps. Dark spaces and shadows that I can't seem to shine a light on." Alice looked thoughtful as she swung her boots back and forth. Mary Shelley rested her head on Alice's lap.

"You don't remember Snuffles at all, do you?" I asked.

"I've told you, Frank, if I could see Snuffles, maybe I would. There were lots of foundlings at IFH," she said sadly.

Snuffles snorted at that and tore through the room, making all the light fixtures flicker and tumbling the books off the top shelf of the bookcase. Mom yelped and Papi got to his feet. My own stomach churned. *Be cool, Snuffles. We're trying,* I begged silently.

"Now, now," Pop-Pop said, "let's all settle down." He

grabbed Papi's wrist and tugged him back into his seat, and Snuffles seemed to mind what Pop-Pop said, too.

Like Alice, I wished I knew what Snuffles looked like. I had a hard time picturing all those kids on the island, picking fruit, playing jump rope, but also missing or grieving their parents. I could almost see and hear them if I closed my eyes. *Memories,* I thought. I imagined all the memories of the world piercing through time, reminding all of us in the present about them, whispering, *Don't forget us.*

Pop-Pop asked more questions after that, like what the weather had been like when I'd first met Alice, or if I could recall the time of day or what I was wearing.

"One more question. Tell me, sonny boy. What monster roams the forest?"

"Let me think," I said. What was Pop-Pop getting at? Did he think Snuffles was a *monster?*

"A Franken-pine!" Pop-Pop guffawed, tricking me. "Just lightening the mood a bit. Y'all were very serious." Mom rolled her eyes.

I couldn't help it. I laughed, too. It was good to have my grandfather with us. It really felt like Spectacle Key was home when he was around. "Pop-Pop, stay here forever, okay?" I asked.

"Will do," Pop-Pop exclaimed, nudging me with his elbow.

Alice giggled, adding, "I could live here forever with you, too, Frank. You'd be like the brother I never had."

I wanted to tell Alice that I'd be the happiest kid alive if we could always be friends. I'd never have to worry about being lonely again.

I was about to say all this when she shrieked, "Ouch, something bit me!" She clamped her hand on her wrist, and when she lifted it, there was a moon-shaped mark on her skin, teeth marks and everything, like she'd had a run-in with that one biting kid in every day-care class.

"What the—" Mom started to ask, but that's when we all heard a deafening roar, like the sound of ten thousand lions waking up at once. We turned and watched through the window behind Alice as a massive wave formed in the distance. Second by second, the wave expanded, until it seemed to blot out the sky.

"Up!" Papi yelled, and we all took off toward the stairs. Outside, the wave seemed to have a voice—a growling, rumbling, SNIFFLING voice.

"Snuffles, no!" Alice was shouting as she ran, but we watched through all the windows as the wave continued to grow. The sky had darkened, too, and it suddenly felt like the middle of the night. A fierce wind yanked fruit off the trees, which pelted the lighthouse. Pelicans, seagulls, and tiny sparrows screeched in the sky, trying to escape the wave.

Mary Shelley howled and howled, like a wolf during a full moon.

"You promised! Abandoned! Forgotten!" sounded a voice in the air that was so deep and horrible I felt it in my bones, rattling me through and through. "You're happy without me, but I haven't been happy in so loooong!"

"We're trying, Snuffles! We're trying!" I kept saying, though I couldn't hear myself above the noise of the wave.

SNIFF! went the wave.

Mom reached the top of the lighthouse first. She held out life jackets for me and Alice, Papi, and Pop-Pop. We watched out the window as the wave crashed against the island, the water coming right up to our front door and washing away Papi's barbecue, our van, and Pop-Pop's car. Luckily, Pop-Pop had brought his things in from the car earlier and had stored some of it on the top floor of the lighthouse.

Mom turned on the television that Papi had set up near the Fresnel lamp to keep him entertained while he repaired it.

The meteorologist for the Keys, Nadia Penwood, was shouting frantically at the camera. Her hair was a mess, and she had no makeup on. She'd probably been dragged to the studio the moment radar picked up the storm. "There is a category five hurricane headed directly toward Spectacle Key," she half shouted. "I repeat. A destructive, life-threatening hurricane is making a beeline toward Spectacle Key. The neighboring keys are not in the cone of danger."

Papi said, "That's impossible! You can see a cat five coming a week in advance!"

"And they're usually huge!" Mom added.

"When you live on Spectacle Key, you've got to believe the impossible," Alice said.

The meteorologist stepped right up to the camera and spoke to my family directly.

"To the brave souls who live on Spectacle Key—stay put!"

I said what we were all thinking. "Snuffles."

"Snuffles," Alice confirmed.

"Frank, if you've made any progress on remembering this out-of-control memory, now would be a good time," Pop-Pop said, but I could only shake my head. Alice and I had planned to return to the library the next day and do more research. But Snuffles wasn't giving us any more time.

From atop the lighthouse, we watched as the bridge to the island got battered by wave after wave, until it eventually washed away.

"So much for help arriving from off the key," Mom said. The electricity cut out and the TV zapped off. Mom lit candles so that we could see. The top floor of the lighthouse was where we kept the hurricane supplies, so we had batteries, water, canned food, and solar-powered cell phone chargers.

The storm raged on and on. It seemed that Snuffles had had enough of waiting for us to remember them properly. We watched as what was left of the Island Foundling Home was swept out to sea, leaving behind only the tiled floor. The coconut palms bent parallel to the ground, bowing like citizens before a king. The tent from the zoning meeting, looking like it had traveled the world, came out of nowhere and flew past the top of the lighthouse.

"I wish we could help, Snuffles. I'm so sorry. So sorry!"

I said as twists of sand flew up like DNA into the sky, then battered the lighthouse so that the sand wedged itself between the bricks.

Mom's cell phone rang and she answered it on speakerphone.

It was Mama Z. "Any chance that you've gotten the lighthouse lamp to work? There's a ship near you that's going to crash ashore any minute now! They've been calling my office for help." In the distance we could hear tinny voices shouting, "Mayday! Mayday!" For the first time since I'd known her, Mama Z sounded panicky.

We all crowded the windows to watch in horror as a speedboat fought against the waves, its bow pointed directly at Spectacle Key's rocky coast. Mom and Papi got to work on the lamp at once, pulling at different wires and checking fuses. "There's nothing wrong with it," Papi was saying. "The thing just refuses to work!"

"Stubborn lamp!" Mom shouted at the lens, banging on it with the palm of her hand.

I knew it wasn't the lamp, or Mom's and Papi's skills. It was Snuffles. In their anger and sadness, Snuffles had lashed out. I wondered if Snuffles had watched the lighthouse from their room at the IFH, if they'd watched it glowing the day they'd been left behind to face a storm alone. Was that why Snuffles was so angry at the lighthouse? At us?

Mary Shelley paced around the lamp, going in circles with Bernard clutched in her jaws. She was nervous, too.

Each time she passed by Alice, Alice gave the dog a kiss on the top of her head.

"Now wait a minute, dog," Pop-Pop said, and tugged on Mary Shelley's collar, stopping her circular route. "I've seen that doll before!" Pop-Pop announced, pulling on Bernard's leg to examine it.

"I found it in the ruin," I explained. "Possibly haunted."

Pop-Pop snapped his fingers and started digging into one of his boxes. "I know it's in here somewhere. I'd been meaning to show you sometime, sonny boy. These are my treasures. Let me see . . . ," he muttered, pulling out signed baseballs, a graduation cap, his diplomas, a baby shoe, a cutting board shaped like Florida, and finally, an old photo album. Outside, the wind made a crying sound, while a blanket flapped like a manta ray past the windows.

Mary Shelley whined for Bernard, and Pop-Pop let the doll go. He sat down on the floor and opened up the photo album. "I know I've seen that thing somewhere." The pages were full of black-and-white photographs. "Our ancestors, see?" Pop-Pop was saying. "There!" He pointed at a torn photograph of a little boy with dark hair, wearing a sailor's outfit. And in his arms was . . .

"Bernard! That boy is holding Bernard!" I shouted.

"Goodness gracious," Alice said, leaning in for a closer look. She reached into her apron and pulled out the picture of herself and her momma. "I didn't put this one back in the files we gave to Manny. Couldn't bear to part with Momma."

Alice handed me the photograph, and I placed it beside the one in Pop-Pop's book. The torn edges matched up precisely. Suddenly, the boy with the sailor doll and Alice and her momma looked like . . . a family. Alice was one of my ancestors! I couldn't believe it. That meant that the little boy holding Bernard was probably one of my ancestors, too.

"Alice, who's this? Do you remember him?"

Alice concentrated hard, closing her eyes and clutching at her temples. "I want to. He's important to me, I can tell. I can feel it here," she said, and pressed a hand over her heart.

Suddenly, we heard a voice clear as crystal cutting through the noise of the storm: "You're so close! *SNIFF!* I'm here, I'm here!"

"Snuffles! Where are you?" I asked. Mom and Papi stopped working on the lamp. Out at sea, the boat, blinded by the waves, came closer to the shore.

"I'm here. I've always been here. Trapped here. Forgotten here! Nameless here!" Snuffles cried.

Pop-Pop gulped. "That voice! I've heard that voice before," he said.

"Me too!" Mom cried. Mom looked all around, searching for the source of the sound.

"Speak the name of the lost child!" Snuffles was saying, while all around the island, the hurricane ripped into trees, devastating everything in its path. In the distance, away from Spectacle Key, the skies were blue and the winds were calm.

"Buster?" Pop-Pop asked, tears in his eyes. "Buster, I haven't heard your voice in a long time."

Snuffles cried and cried.

"Oh, it breaks my heart, Frank," Alice said, clutching my T-shirt. "Why can't I remember?"

Snuffles had been Pop-Pop's imaginary friend! Mom's, too! He'd been haunting members of my family now for three generations, begging us to remember him. Pop-Pop and Mom were from the Florida Keys. This place had always been home to them, and I suppose it was home to me, Alice, and Snuffles, too.

"Pop-Pop, what do you know about these kids?" I asked, pointing at the picture.

Pop-Pop scratched his chin. "Heaps of folks I don't know in that album. My great-great-grandparents had nineteen children. Couldn't ever keep track of all those relatives."

Snuffles howled and the candles went out in a puff of smoke all at once. "Pop-Pop, you have to remember!" I shouted. Meanwhile, Papi and Mom were back at the lamp, cursing at the tools and each other while the boat at sea barreled toward craggy rocks.

"My granny told me the story of cousins who were sent to an orphanage long ago. Nobody ever talked about them. I think they felt bad. Don't recall her ever speaking their names, if she even knew them. Like I said, it was a long, long time ago, and there were lots of people in the family tree."

"So our family forgot them?" I asked in horror.

Pop-Pop nodded. "I believe so. Forgotten. Terrible thing to happen to people."

"Come find me!" Snuffles shrieked, louder than ever. "I'm here, I'm here."

"Maybe there's something written on the back." I popped the picture out of the little black corners that held the torn photo in place. Trembling, I turned it over. There, written in blue ink, was a pair of names and ages—Alice Gale, age 10, and Albert Gale, age 7.

Nervously, I looked at Alice.

"My brother," she gasped. Alice squinched her eyes tight, and when she opened them she breathed out, "I remember." She fell to the floor, her knees buckling from under her. "It was the three of us—me, Albert, and Momma. Then my momma got sick and she brought us here, to Spectacle Key. When the hurricane came, Albert and I were napping upstairs. When we woke up, everybody was gone. The wind came first. Then the waves. I tried to hold on to Albert, but it was dark, the dead of night, and the water was so high." Alice covered her face with her hands.

"Alice, where are you?" Snuffles howled.

"I remember you! Please don't be mad at me. I'm a memory, too, after all!" she shouted to her brother. Then Alice looked at me, her eyes red-rimmed and wide. "This has to be it, Frank. Speak his name. Someone living has to remember him," she said.

I gathered myself, holding the picture close to my chest,

and bellowed, "Your name is Albert Gale! You aren't forgotten anymore! I promise you'll be remembered from now on!"

Suddenly, the lamp turned on in a blinding blaze. We closed our eyes against the brightness, which left tiny, dancing suns in my vision for a while. Outside, the boat turned away. The waves it had bobbed on like a toy were calming by the second. Bit by bit, the skies lightened, until it was dry and calm outside. The hurricane had dissipated like smoke.

"Increíble," gushed Papi.

"Amazing," whispered Mom.

"Well, I'll be," said Pop-Pop.

There, standing beside Alice, was Albert. We could all see them both now, clear as a picture.

"Bertie," Alice sighed, and took hold of Albert's hands. "I remember you now. You always beat everybody at marbles. You loved candy, all kinds. And the Trembly sisters took Bernard from you and locked him away in a cupboard. You cried for weeks."

Sheepish, Albert lowered his face. "Hi, Alice. I'm sorry I caused so much trouble. I missed you and Momma so much." He was only a little boy and his voice was small and squeaky.

"Oh!" Alice cried, hugging her brother. "Me too, me too, me too," she kept saying, and rocked him in her arms.

My mom whispered, "My word," while Papi made the sign of the cross over himself and muttered something I didn't catch in Spanish.

Pop-Pop came forward with his hand out. Albert shook

it, smiling. His front teeth were missing. His face had freckles all over and he looked a lot like Alice, actually. "Science can't explain everything now, can it?" Pop-Pop said, then added, "It's good to know your name, Albert. Though I'll always think of you as Buster."

Albert gave Pop-Pop a hug and then gave one to Mom, too. She told him, "Hello, my not-so-imaginary friend. I've missed you. I'm so glad you aren't sad anymore."

"I'm happy now," said Albert. "You have a nice family, Joyce, and you're so grown up. I wish kids didn't have to grow up. I would have been your friend always." Mom wiped the tears from her eyes. "If you hadn't come here," Albert said, "me and Alice might've been lost forever. Thank you."

"You're welcome," my mom whispered.

Finally, Albert faced me. "You've been a real pal, Frank."

"I'm nobody's pal," I said. It was true. I hadn't ever had a friend who lasted very long. The only real friend I'd ever had was just a memory.

Albert said, "Look around. Alice and me wouldn't be here without your help. You've remembered us, and I'm sure you'll figure out a way to help others remember us, too."

"He's right," Alice said. "You and your family, I mean, *our family,* mended me and Albert. We were broken and forgotten before."

I tried not to cry and did a good job of it, mostly. It made my throat hurt, though. We heard birds chirping outside, and fluffy white clouds floated in the blue sky, as if nothing had happened. The IFH was totally gone, though, which maybe was for the best. It really hadn't been a safe place to play. Papi and Mom stared out at the now wide-open space.

"A museum would look great over there. A small one, commemorating the IFH and the children who lost their lives in the hurricane," Papi said, his eyes bright and glassy, the way they always got when he went into building planning mode.

"With a playground for the children on the neighboring keys, of course," Mom added.

"And a dog park?" I put in, thinking of how much fun Mary Shelley would have meeting dog pals of her own.

"Alice," Albert said, interrupting. "You know we have to go, right?"

Alice smiled. "I know," she said. When Alice wrapped me in a hug that knocked the breath out of me, I started to cry for real. "Frank, I'll miss you so much," she said. "You'll always be my bestest friend. But I know you'll make new ones. And you'll make lots of new memories to keep forever."

"I'll never forget you, Alice," I managed to croak out.

Mary Shelley trotted over to Albert with Bernard in her mouth. She dropped it wetly at his feet. Albert chuckled. "You can keep him." Mary Shelley must have understood, because she scooped up Bernard and took off down the stairs with it, the toy officially hers at last.

"Goodbye, Frank. I know how to spell it now," Albert said.

"Thanks. Here," I said, pulling out a small pack of gummy bears from my pocket and handing them to Albert.

"I love candy!" Albert said.

"I know." I got sad thinking that the air on Spectacle Key might not smell as sweet now that Albert and Alice were leaving for good. I took a deep breath and felt myself getting braver. We'd done a good thing, Alice and me. But it still hurt to say goodbye. "Bye, Albert," I said.

"Cousin Albert to you."

"Cousin Albert," I echoed, a knot in my throat.

As for Alice, there was nothing else for us to say. Her cheeks were shiny with tears and mine were, too. She waved, then held her brother's hand. Together they went down the winding lighthouse stairs. I watched them go, and the last thing I saw was the back of her T-shirt and the words *See you later, alligator.*

Chapter 26

THE GROUP AT CENTRAL KEYS MIDDLE SCHOOL

"First day of sixth grade," Mom sang while packing my lunch. I'd refused to get a new lunchbox. That was for elementary school kids. I was a middle schooler now, so I'd brown bag it. I had a plain blue backpack and was wearing my new school uniform—khaki shorts and a green polo shirt with the logo for Central Keys Middle School on it.

I rode to school with Papi, who chattered on about the construction of the IFH museum. He and Mom had received a grant from HAUNT, as well as a flower arrangement and a note of apology from Ms. Emily Shiverton, who ended her Flippy campaign early (the Flippy vote happened later that month and Manny the acrobatic librarian won!). SCARE was providing plants for a museum garden, and the guys in SADS promised to do an exhibit on cryptids, featuring the Swamp Ape! Mama Z came by the job site often, giving advice and helping the permit process move along in her role as mayor. Fernández Home Conversions was only doing consultations now, and Mom and Papi helped homeowners across the country convert all kinds of wild buildings into family homes, all from the comfort of our lighthouse.

All in all, the Fernández family had finally settled for good on Spectacle Key.

Things really did calm down once Alice and Albert were properly remembered. Work on restoring the lighthouse moved quickly—there were no more invasive crabs or superpowered vines, scary weather events, broken appliances, or missing tools. The best thing of all was that Mom and Papi stopped arguing. Sure, they'd sometimes bicker the way most parents do, but they were also so lovey-dovey it made me want to puke.

I wouldn't change a thing.

As for Pop-Pop, he taught me all there was to know about tide pools and the creatures that lived in them, and the things he did with that old chemistry set blew my mind. In return, I told him all about my favorite books, and he let me read to him most nights, the two of us huddled together on my twin-sized bed while Mary Shelley and Bernard snuggled on the floor.

Summer on Spectacle Key was great.

But I missed Alice. I missed her laugh, her freckles, her hopefulness, her teasing, her rummaging through my

T-shirts, her old-fashioned dress and red-laced boots, and the way she had believed in me. I didn't think I'd ever stop missing her. Maybe it was a good thing. You can't ever forget a person who you miss, and there was no way I'd ever forget Alice, or Albert.

After a short drive, Papi pulled into the school drop-off lane and stopped the van. "Good luck today, Frank."

"Thanks, Papi!" I said. I gripped the handle of the door, but before I stepped out, I asked, "We're still staying, right? The friends I make here I get to keep for real?"

Papi's eyes got a little shiny. "Mi hijito, I promise this with all my heart. We are home. Go make new buddies, okay?"

I laughed. "Sí, Papi," I said, then headed into school.

Inside, the school was a bustling, bright, happy place. Kids shouted and greeted one another, showing off new backpacks and sneakers. Like in the rest of the Keys, the decor was loud and tropical. The walls were painted over in ocean murals, including the lockers. My locker, number 950, had a sea turtle's face on it. I was just loading my notebooks into it when I felt a tap on my shoulder.

"Hey, Frank," said Lucas. He looked nervous, chewing the inside of his cheek as he stood there.

"Hey," I said. I wondered how much everyone in the Keys knew about his mom and all she'd done to keep their dark family secret. Ms. Shiverton was trying to make amends, though, by helping with the museum, and I hoped people knew that about her, too. "I'm sorry I was weird this summer," I said at last when the silence between us grew a little uncomfortable. I felt bad for assuming Lucas had been playing a prank on me when he just wanted to be friends.

"I'm sorry, too. It was just that—a very weird summer," Lucas said.

I agreed. He had no idea, in fact. "So what's up?" I asked him.

Lucas broke into a big grin. "I'm glad you're here. Wanna meet my friends?"

I nodded, shoved the rest of my notebooks and supplies in my locker, set the lock, and followed Lucas into an outdoor courtyard. He stopped and scanned the place, which was full of picnic tables and potted palms, and finally found what he was looking for—a picnic table where six other kids sat. They waved him over.

"Everybody, meet Frank," Lucas said. "Frank, this is Annika, Victoria, Ámbar, Lorenzo, Oliver, and Demi."

"Hey," I said, suddenly feeling out of breath. It would take me a while to remember all those names. Then I realized I had a whole school year to get them straight. Scratch that—we weren't moving again. Happiness washed over me like a sweet breeze. I'd have all of middle school to get to know lots of kids!

"Scooch over for the new guy," the girl named Victoria announced, patting the seat next to her.

"Thanks," I said. Victoria had brown eyes and freckles

like Alice's, and when she talked about her language arts class, she gushed about the summer reading assignment while the others groaned.

"Well, I loved it, and that's that," Victoria said, crossing her arms.

"I did, too," I added.

"There. See? At least one of you in the group reads!" Victoria said with a laugh.

Me. In a group. I could hardly believe it. I looked at Lucas and gave him a big smile, and he gave me one back.

When the bell rang, I followed Lucas and the others to our first-period class, which happened to be language arts. The teacher had placed paper on each of the desks. Printed at the top was *What did you learn this summer?*

"Children! Welcome," she announced. "My name is Ms. Yamanaka. I believe we are all curious and that because of our curiosity, we are learning every moment of our lives. So before we do anything else, please teach me something I might not know!"

I glanced to my right. Victoria got straight to work. I took a peek at her page and it looked like she'd started writing about monarch butterflies. To my left, Lucas sat staring at the ceiling, then he gasped and wrote *Mastering Video Games This Summer* at the top of his page. I hid a laugh. Inside I felt all fluttery. They were happy, warm flutters.

It was a feeling Alice had once called *peace*.

I pulled out my favorite pencil. Ms. Yamanaka wanted to

learn about something she didn't know? Well, I had a story to tell and a promise to keep, after all.

So I began by writing:

Albert and Alice Gale: The Lost (and Found!) Children of Spectacle Key

ACKNOWLEDGMENTS

The book you are holding was written during a worldwide pandemic. Being able to escape to the Florida Keys with Frank, Mary Shelley, his parents, and the friends he makes on the island was the best kind of self-care. Part of what the pandemic shone a light on (not unlike a lighthouse's life-saving beam!) was the importance of science and scientific discovery. Frank is a scientist-in-the-making, and in his way, helped along by a bit of magic and mystery, he's leaving his world a better place than he found it. May we all do our part in this, in whatever way we can.

So, thank you to scientists everywhere. This book is an ode to you and all that you do in the service of helping others.

I am forever grateful for my editor, Kristin Rens, for loving Frank and his friends right from the beginning. It's a miracle to find another person in the world who gets what your imagination is trying to do, and Kristin totally does, every time.

Big thanks to the whole team at Balzer + Bray, for the care they put into this novel, and the work they do to put wonderful books for children out into the world.

Thank you to my agent, Stéphanie Abou, for joining me on adventures on the page and off. Frank found a kindred spirit in Connie, just as I found one in you, querida Stéphanie. Gracias por todo.

Thank you to Las Musas collective for your support and the efforts you put toward representing and highlighting Latinos in kidlit. My own children and countless others see themselves in books thanks to important efforts like yours.

Para la pandilla Tangier, los chicos y los grandes, ya saben quienes son. Gracias por su amistad en esta época tan emocionante.

To my extended family—a massively grateful hug for all that you do. Tita would be so proud of us.

To my mom, a tough cookie who introduced scary movies to me when I was a kid: if this book makes readers jump a little, it's thanks to your influence! To my dad, thank you for being the real-life Pop-Pop to my kids. Love you both!

To my daughters, Penelope and Mary-Blair, this book is for you. They're all for you. Thank you for the joy you bring me every day. I love you.

And finally, love always to my husband, Orlando, the coolest scientist I know. My hero, you make the world a better place in every way.